SAJESH SHAKYA

What Should I Do

When History Repeats itself in the Worst Way

Contents

What Should I Do

When History Repeats Itself in the Worst Ways

One

My lovely wife was working on her laptop. Her legs warm under the blanket while her fingers ran a marathon on the keyboard. My phone vibrated inside my pocket. I took it out and saw that I had just received a text.

It's him, I thought, my mouth drying. The person that might lead me to make a severe change in my life. I made an excuse and scurried to the bathroom, away from prying eyes.

"I know you're a grown man and so I shouldn't be saying this but still. Don't take too long playing some stupid game, Dave," my wife said. "I better not hear any cheap gunshot sounds from here," Kate warned.

"Okay, dear," I wanted to say that I hadn't played any games in weeks, but I didn't. I just faked a half-assed smile and closed the door behind me. I double checked, making sure I had locked it well, not that I was worried she might barge in. She was way too comfortable where she was. I walked around and took quick deep breaths before I unlocked my phone to see what was in the inbox.

"You bring the money. I bring the information. I'll send in the address. See you tomorrow," the text read, in four individual sentences all put together like a list.

I replied, agreeing to his conditions, in just one word, "OK". *Fingers crossed.*

Ten minutes later, I was back on the bed, with Kate. She stretched her arms, the way she always did after finishing her project for the day. She yawned, opening her mouth big and wide. For a second there I pictured my hand forcing itself inside her, all the way into her throat. Pushing further down, going deeper, until I felt her tiny little heart with my fingers and pressed in.

She turned off the light on her side and laid down, not facing me, not that I cared. I couldn't sleep but I tried. I put my glasses on the bedside table. My head resting on the soft pillow, which due to the thoughts that were running in my head, was as comfortable as a skinny cat's rotten corpse.

My wife turned towards me, her eyebrows raised as she gestured towards the light on my side of the bed, signaling me to turn it off.

She doesn't know what I'm thinking, I thought, and gave her a quick smile as I rolled out of her reach and turned off the light. I smiled again in the darkness and pulled up the covers up to my chest, like a good boy. I tried to shake off the negative thoughts that usually kept me awake.

Just a false alarm, I told myself, reassuring the notion that this small family of ours was safe and happy, and would remain that way. That life isn't as cruel as it once used to be. 'Like father like son' has always been the worst case scenario in my mind and will always remain that way. I'm not sure how or if I'll be able to handle it if it does come to fruition.

The room was now completely dark and, other than our breathing noises, silent as well. Yet it still took me hours to actually fall asleep. Usually by this time, my daily sleep routine would just force me to close my eyes and get some much needed shut eye. It hadn't failed me in almost a decade, until now.

Anxiety kept me awake. The stress of not knowing what tomorrow could bring kept my mind too preoccupied to listen to the rest of my body. Funny how sometimes your body can go against you.

When I woke up, it felt as if I had barely slept an hour, which made sense since, according to my alarm clock, that was all the rest I got.

Funny how sometimes your body can go against you.

Two

With a quick goodbye kiss on my lips, Kate finally left the apartment.

"Take care," I tell her, holding back several curses that my mind had produced in the last hour.

"You too," she nodded, barely even looking at me. She was probably holding back her side of curses too. *What else could she be thinking? If she didn't hate me, she wouldn't have done what she did, but did she? The nightmare continues...*

I looked out the window, waiting for her car to leave the building. It wasn't there yet. I backed off a little and grabbed a glass of cold water as I waited. It was better, refreshing even and helped my breathing. Which in turn helped me remain calm and not turn the whole room into a mess. Although, temptation did try to intervene.

I damn near broke the glass once I was done drinking. The small yet audible crack of the glass on my hand stopped me before I could go all the way and hurt myself, again. *Unleashing the beast inside could do me no favors.*

I turned off the lights and pulled the curtains closed, hoping to convince the world outside that there was no one home. Although I doubt anyone would be watching to begin with. Still I used the bright grass green curtains as a cover and hid behind them. Making my way to the very edge, I sneaked a peak out again.

It took forever before Kate finally drove out the gate. I checked the time again, almost 11 am. I told Kate that I would see her later, as you do, but what I didn't say however, was that I'd be skipping work today. Convincing my boss that I was feeling under the weather was easier than expected. Yet keeping that same information away from Kate was… uncomfortable to say the least. Like I was betraying her. But then I forced myself to recall the reason I was actually doing it, and it made it feel justified, even if just a little.

Once confirmed that she was gone, I got ready to head out myself. I dressed in casual jeans, which were tighter than the last time I wore them. Back when Kate and I were going through a little depression session. I've put on weight. I got in my car, the driver seat colder than usual. *Maybe this is all just an overreaction. Maybe I'm worrying too much. Maybe I'm just wrong. And if I am wrong, I… I guess I'll just confess everything to her.* I'm man enough to admit when I've fucked up.

She deserves to know what I did, but only what I did, not what I thought about her during the whole time I suspected her. I love her to death and I always will, but during the last few days, I found out the frightening truth that I can also hate her just as much if I needed to. I don't want to need that, not now, not ever.

With sweaty palms on the steering wheel and my heart beating rapidly in my chest, I drove for half an hour to the address he sent me. I could never spell or even pronounce the name of these cheap foreign cafés so I was sent a picture. Like Kate once said, *GPS is one of the best inventions ever.* It seems I agree.

I stopped and parked my car across the street, right in front of the café he chose. I double checked the image and concluded that I was indeed at the right place. I didn't need to have any doubts about it, but for some reason I did. Maybe I was hoping to be at the wrong place.

I got out of the car and the sharp sunlight pierced my skin like needles. God, it was hot. I should not have worn jeans. It felt like I was inside an oven and covered in oil.

My phone buzzed inside my pocket right when I was about to jump back in. *Another text.* 'Come in,' it said. He's around, he's probably watching me from a distance. There was nothing else for me to do. So I walked towards the Café and got inside at once. Cold gentle air from the AC above welcomed me as warm crimson lights bounced off my t-shirt. The fresh smell of coffee made my mouth water. I welcomed the sudden shift in atmosphere as it was fresh and relaxing, I needed that, more than I care to admit.

Whenever I visit a restaurant or café of any kind, and the aroma hits, I buy a cup. It works every time. Then I would sit by the window and look at the street, or garden, depending on where I'm at. That's how I normally enjoy my beverage, but today was far from being a normal day.

For the last few days, I haven't been able to recall exactly how a normal day even feels like. I miss those good old times. Back when Kate and I would have long drawn out conversations about our jobs and colleagues. How the new lawyers were lectured for gossiping about their clients, how they depended on the firm a little too much and I'll add in my own experience of how my colleague Suzan's kid made a drawing of a building that looked like a dick. One of her female friends even commented, "Aww look, little Johnny drew exactly the type of building his mommy likes," Suzan blushed at the comment and we laughed even harder. *Good times.*

"Excuse me," A lady's voice snapped back to reality. The voice came from behind and realized I was standing still by the door. I quickly moved out of the way. I had unknowingly been blocking her, along with the toddler who was in her arms. I whispered a small sorry that even I couldn't hear well as I walked towards the window and next to a wall, away from anyone's path.

From there, I skimmed the room for him. Maybe it's because I haven't been to any cheap cafés in years or maybe I just underestimated the appeal these restaurants have but I did not expect a café like this to be as crowded as it was, especially at this time of the day. Some of them were obviously just teenagers with no income on a date. The rest were mostly middle aged women. The kind of women who don't have any jobs of their own, other than being housewives. There were some men here and there but none of them were the person I was looking for.

It must've taken me a while to spot him, as a skinny arm jumped out from the crowd, impatient or maybe in a hurry. I barely saw it at first and even when I did notice it, I almost ignored it, thinking it wasn't for me, until he raised his other arm which caught my attention. The ugly snake tattoo on his hand gave me his identification and I made my way towards his table.

He was sitting in the far side of a corner all the way to the left, like one of those students in a classroom who doesn't want to be noticed by the teacher as he writes 'fuck' in capital letters on the desk, thinking how cool he is. As I got closer I became more grateful that he had chosen this spot. The noise from the crowd was almost completely gone by the time I saw the menu on the table. This was clearly not his first time meeting a client here. He might as well be a regular for all I care.

"Nice place," I said. He gave a small, barely noticeable shrug and gestured to me to sit on the empty seat right in front of him, which I did. He took a massive bite from his chocolate muffin and picked up his drink as I looked at the menu without paying any attention to whatever they had in it. Food was the last of my concerns. My stomach can wait, my mind and heart can't.

"Got the money?" he asked through a muffled voice as he sipped his latte, getting a bit of yellow under his thick black mustache as he did so. I hate it when people talk while their mouth is still full. *Just swallow it*, I want to scream at them, but I don't. Unlike them I haven't lost my manners.

He had a stupid old brown hat that looked like it belonged to someone's grandfather, maybe his own, and wore glasses that seemed like they had been knocked out of his face on more than one occasion. He looked more like Charlie Chaplin than a private detective. *I didn't hire the most capable guy, did I?* Then again he was said to be reliable, safe, and surprisingly cheap, just what I needed, but not wanted.

"Only if you've got what I need," he nodded and put his hand inside his jacket. He wiped off the mess on his mustache with his sleeve like a little boy as he pulled out an envelope. He jerked it back in when I tried to reach for it.

"You got the check?" I shook my head and put my hand inside my pocket. *I got something better.* I pulled out a different envelope, a longer one, with cash in it and gave it to him. My envelope was clearly heavier than his. He took it but didn't open it. At least he wasn't that dumb. *Did he seriously think I was going to give him a check? Did I hire an amateur?* I sighed and focused on the envelope instead. It was way too late to think about the rest.

"Should I open it here or at home?" I asked, hoping the news was good even though by that point it was more wishful thinking, than logical. Even if it was just a misunderstanding, which I hoped it was, she wouldn't like it when I evidently tell her, which I will. I won't blame her if she gets too upset and even slaps me. I would let her throw me out the window for having done such a thing, as long as she doesn't leave me.

"You can open it wherever you want to, but if you ask me, home is what I'd recommend, far from anyone and everyone. That way if you feel like breaking something, you don't have to worry about all the eyes that'll be on you," I nodded as I opened it just slightly, only to peek inside a little, and to check that these were indeed what I had asked for, what I hired him for. Maybe he was a professional, just with terrible fashion sense, who preferred to look like pink panther more than James bond. I put it in my jacket pocket. Unsure if I should leave right away or talk to him some more.

"Now we're done," he whispered, loud enough for me to hear, and went back to his meal like there was no tomorrow. *If he was more capable at his job than he looked, then it was money well spent.*

"Yes," I nodded as he put my money in his pocket. *Wait, why did he imply I might feel like breaking something? Was the news bad?* I thought but couldn't bring myself to ask. He didn't fake a reassuring smile either, like the way he did back when we first met, which stung more than it should have.

Funny how sometimes you have to pay certain people to ruin your life. What's worse is that if this work of his was accurate to my suspicions, then I'd have to pay even more money to worsen the nightmare I'd been living with for weeks, *a therapy*. It's like paying the devil to let me know that hell is indeed real and then charging me an additional entrance fee.

We shook hands and I stood up, ready to leave. I looked at his face a while longer before I left and what I saw hurt me. A sympathetic smile appeared on his face, the worst indicator that, yes, *I'm fucked*. A month or so earlier, when I had paid him the advance, he had been more transparent. He'd been fake, which made him easier to read. He faked a look that said, don't worry, everything's going to be fine.

Now that he already knew the result I wanted so desperately to know, he was being unintentionally real with his emotions. It felt like getting stabbed. He must've noticed how I felt as he mouthed a silent, sorry. It didn't help. I broke the brief eye contact we just had as my eyes started to well up. I quickly walked out of the café, stumbling like a jackass as tears slowly filled up my eyes and I struggled to hold them in. On my way I bumped into a high school couple that just walked in, nearly tackling the guy to the ground. Another inaudible sorry as I rushed out. "Watch where you're going asshole!" he said. I half expected the guy to come at me but he didn't.

I was so quick that even the strong smell of caffeine went almost unnoticed. I wiped my tears, breathing hard as I did so. For a second there I forgot where I was until I looked back at the café and the people inside, I stood still for just a millisecond, before turning back around as I headed to my car, avoiding a near miss from a bike. The biker yelled something at me that I heard but didn't understand or cared.

I opened the door to my car and threw myself on the seat. The whole car bounced a little as I did so. I wiped the tears off my glasses with a tissue. My heart beating faster as time passed. I wasn't sure if I should check the envelope or drive home. I chose the latter. I put my glasses back on and started the car. Driving home would be safer if I was in the right headspace, which was putting it mildly.

Since I had decided not to open the packet unless I was inside the house, I turned it into an excuse. I basically spent half an hour driving to nowhere. I no longer wanted to go home, or anywhere. I just drove senselessly and circled the same block several times, over and over again until I heard my stomach rumble.

Fuck! *Should've had a bigger breakfast.* I wasn't hungry then and now I regretted it. However I still didn't want to stop. I checked the fuel to see how long I can still drive. I didn't notice it before but just like luck, I was running out of it as well. I took a deep long breath and decided it'll be best to get it over with. I can't keep running away from my fate. I can no longer delay the inevitable.

On my way home, for real this time, I saw a bar. A well decorated 'newly opened' sign hung on the glass door. I haven't had a drink in a year, an occasional beer or wine but nothing too hard, rehabilitation.

Under the normal circumstances I would stay that way, but today was way past normal. I bought a large bottle of whiskey; the bottle itself was far heavier than the actual drink. I know it shouldn't have surprised me but for some reason it did. I wanted to open it immediately but I didn't. It may come in handy later, when I evidently open the envelope.

Three

I parked my car closer to the elevator than where I usually would. If I could, I would've driven all the way to my room as well. I jumped out of my car and rushed inside the elevator as soon as it opened. I pushed the buttons to my floor, only push isn't the correct word. It was more like a punch but with fingers and several buttons at once, not sure if I even touched the one I needed to.

When the doors closed in front of me, I was quickly overtaken by the urge to kick the metal walls staring at me, trapping me. I didn't kick but I did slam my palms on them, as if trying to push someone from the back. The cold surface of the metal pushed back and I heard a small cling. It was the sound of the wall coming in contact with my ring.

The ring that was so tight that it choked the life out of my finger back when I first wore it. We loved the Tron-like design it had so rather than looking for an alternative, we just resized it. I covered the ring with my other hand, as if it was not to be seen. That was when I realized how badly my hands had been shaking.

With the bottle still in my hand, I wiped a layer of sweat off my forehead and wiped it back on my T-shirt. In the elevator, my head bobbed up and down like a toy. I looked up and waited to get to my floor, then I glanced down again at the bottle in my hand, wondering if I was setting myself up for a disaster. Maybe I was, but my mind was too preoccupied to think of anything else than what I had in my jacket pocket.

I hoped again, for it to be a false alarm, for it to be forgotten as an honest mistake, but my mind was too sure it was not. Surely all the shit that I had been through wasn't going to be for a small misunderstanding, even if a part of me hoped it to be. What the hell? Why do I already sound so sure? Did I want this to happen? Fuck no!

I closed my eyes and recalled the small glimpses of what I saw inside the package, back when I opened it in that restaurant. I had seen only one photograph. It was of Kate, the woman I married, the love of my life, standing out of her firm with her friends, colleagues, and a banker. The banker who she in her own words, once was classmates with. Who she may possibly be more than just friends with now.

I shook the image off my head by hitting myself on the forehead with my fist. As if on impulse, I checked my phone. Where is all the distraction when you need it? It felt like a good time to get notified on YouTube or twitter, or maybe an email, even if spam. Maybe a celebrity died, or was arrested for something illegal. Maybe someone famous got in a fucking car crash. Literally anything would've done, but in the end there was nothing. Nothing that could distract me. I could barely scroll past one Instagram story.

I came across a friend's post about a birthday party for her mom. Her mom was as old as my mom would've been if she were still around. That post just made everything worse. I put the phone back in my pocket, squeezing it so tight I might as well break it, if I was strong enough. My mind was free, and it was a curse, even though it shouldn't have been.

The more I thought about it, the more my head hurt and I felt like falling to the floor. To lie down and take a nap inside the tall electronic cube, but I couldn't. The steel walls suddenly felt more claustrophobic than a second ago as if they were closing in on me like some death trap. *How long have I been here?*

I punched in my floor number, over and over until my finger hurt.

Once the elevator stopped, and the walls started to open, letting in some extra air, I rushed to get out and even hit my shoulders on the edge of the metal doors. The pain was there but I shrugged it off as I made a run for my apartment. No one was there to see me, not that I would've even noticed anyone with all the adrenaline rushing through me. I looked like the teenager who just got home in the middle of the night with meth in his pockets and blood on his knuckles.

Finally I reached my apartment and slammed the door behind me, hard enough for the sound to echo inside. The small yet much needed release of force was satisfying. I wanted to do it again, and again, over and over until the damn door broke off its hinges. But I didn't, I'm way too stressed to handle the angry flock of neighbors that'll come out to complain if I did so.

I headed to the kitchen and jerked the refrigerator door open. I wanted to eat whatever I could find but not just because I was hungry. I searched for the leftover fruits and dinner from yesterday, or any other day. Anything to eat, to distract, to postpone what I really should've been doing, what I feared to be doing.

But it was pointless. The refrigerator was empty. There were a few pieces of spinach and some leftover pizza curling at the edges. Nothing to eat. Nothing to distract me from the inevitable.

A deep breath as I planned the next thing I was going to do. Try to think of it as a Band-Aid, quick and painless. I hoped it was quick but wishing it to be painless felt too far-fetched at this point.

With a large empty glass in my hand, I returned to the living room, right between the kitchen and the bathroom. The empty sofa waited for me to sit down and give up, which I did. Despite my best attempts, it took only a minute to finish the pizza. I even licked the plate it was on and washed it as overtime, but time does not stop for anyone. If anything, it slows down to make it even worse.

I squeezed open the bottle and poured myself a glass. My hand started shaking again as I pulled out the envelope. Deep breath, a small sip of the strong drink to build up some courage, then another deep breath, as I opened it and spread the insides on the small coffee table in front of me.

Dozens of pictures covered the table. Pictures of Kate with the banker next door were what most of them featured, but there were also some with other male colleagues. I grabbed a bunch of the pictures and slowly went through them, analyzing them, making sure I wasn't jumping onto any silly conclusions right away. There sure were many pictures, too many if you ask me.

One had her walk with him to a Starbucks, nothing harmful, just two friends out for a drink, sharing a meal, probably just a friendly get together. The other is in a park, a jog maybe, exercise buddies with benefits. And a picture that was taken from a distance where it was hard to tell if he was even the same person, but what was pretty clear was that the place looked like a cheap motel and the skinny lady was unmistakably my wife.

It looked like it was taken from across the street and without any additional lenses. No wonder he was so cheap, he could barely take a picture right. Quantity over quality seemed to be his motto so far.

There were a bunch of others where she appeared to be just standing, or maybe it was the illusion of the still images, where she was with her colleagues. The ones with the banker had her in mostly restaurants, but she was not alone with him, at least not always.

Most of them looked normal and it helped me breathe better. There was a picture of her with a colleague, whose face was only visible from the side. A blonde with long hair, like one of those Korean hairstyles, a surprisingly long cheekbone and from what I was able to make out, fit enough to be doing daily workouts.

Yet it was the hot shot banker she spent the most time with, almost like a gold digger. If she had cheated on me with the young lawyer, at least I would've felt like she wanted some youth or stamina or whatever the fuck else she could be getting from a younger leaner guy, but a chubby banker? Somehow it was worse. I shook my head and told myself out loud, "Don't jump into conclusions, you dumb fuck."

All these images could be interpreted as friendships. *Did I misread my own source?* But then why would he say 'sorry' if there was nothing harmful to be found? I was clearly worrying over nothing. This may all just be some silly misunderstanding after all.

The next photograph made sure I never reassured myself of it ever again. Just when I started to relax, the next picture removed any chance of misunderstanding. I took off my glasses and rubbed my eyes to make sure what I saw was indeed real and not the alcohol taking its effect.

I put my glasses back on, even though my eyes aren't that bad, and try to breathe. The photo I held in my hand, featured my wife, and only part of the guy. This was taken from a distance and it was quite dark, maybe a storeroom, or maybe at the cheap motel. The only source of light was a big ass lamp right next to the bed, in front of her. It was taken from the other side of an old windowpane, but the image was still clear enough to destroy my life.

The man in the picture was sitting, that's all I could make out of the man. Well, that and his dick inside my wife's mouth, as she gave a familiar naughty smile that was once reserved for me. The room itself seemed dim but Kate however was, quite visibly, on her knees in front of him. I will recognize those cheeks and that smile anywhere.

The face of the man was blocked, but it didn't matter anymore. If your wife's on her knees sucking someone, the issue shouldn't be that she's on her knees, but the fact that the person who she's sucking, is clearly not you. *Why Kate? Why?*

I checked at the bottom of the picture to see when it was taken. The pictures all had dates on them and most of them were taken during the last three weeks, the times when she had called home, or to me, letting me know that she was going to be late, that there was too much work at the office.

Tears came back to my eyes before I could even get to the next picture. Soon all of the photos were a blur. I collected them all, shuffled them together and went through them all over again. I rubbed my eyes again and again as I did so, making sure my eyes weren't tricking me.

What kind of a fucking imbecile have I hired? The pictures looked like he could barely use the camera. Some were from such poor angles and some from a distance too far. Only a handful of good photos, at best. Maybe I ought to have spied on her myself. "That good for nothing son of a b…" I sigh. Blaming him for his weakness was not going to make me feel better about my own. In the end, it no longer mattered how good or bad he was, at least he got the job done.

Despite the clear lack of quality in the pictures, I had already confirmed what I wanted to know. That's all I'd been worried about. The confirmation that what I feared was indeed true, the nightmare was real and my heart struggled to take it. My chest tightened and it got harder to breathe all of a sudden. The oxygen in the room was not enough for me, I needed some air.

I rushed for the windows and pushed my head out. I blinked a million times as I held back tears and tried to breathe, quickly, heavily, and a lot. There was no one who saw me, or at least no one I could see. I felt like jumping out of the window, and I damn near did.

Now despite all of it, the big question remained. *How do I confront her? Do I yell at her at the top of my lungs or berate her and her lover in public?* I don't think I can do the latter even if I wanted to. What will *he* say? I shook the very thought of him away.

Should I at least let our neighbors know of her infidelity, or do I ask her why she did what she did in a way it's kept just between the two of us, so that I can at least focus and try to understand, as to why she turned into such a fucking whore. After how much I trusted her. After how much I shared with her. How can she possibly justify it?

After enough time had passed, I barged back into the living room and took a sip off the glass, then another. I didn't even realize how much I already drank until my eyelids started to get heavy. That was when I noticed I didn't have my glasses on anymore. They must've fallen out when I was at the window. No wonder everything was so fucking hazy.

I could still make out certain things so I didn't worry much. I dropped the glass on the floor, only dropped wasn't the word. I threw the glass at the wall and it shattered into pieces right next to the TV. I didn't care, I wouldn't have cared even if it hit the damn thing. I stomped on the glass table in front of me, shattering it. Large pieces of it stuck to my leg but I did care.

I grabbed the bottle and started drinking directly from it. The alcohol, the heartache, the headache, I wanted to sit but I couldn't, I wanted to scream but I couldn't, I didn't know what I should do, so I did what seemed to be helping at the moment, I drank, and I kept drinking.

Four

I woke up a few hours later, on the couch, where I last remember sitting and where I still sat. The empty bottle fell from my grip and onto my bleeding foot. Maybe that's what woke me up. Beads of sweat trickled down my nose and onto my jacket. I took it off and noticed that my chest was also covered in a layer of sweat. I looked around but saw nothing. The room was pitch black, or maybe my eyes were telling me to get an extra pair of glasses next time.

Quick glances at the windows told me that the room was dark because the sun had set. I can't remember the last time I slept for this long during a day. Usually I am not a fan of darkness but I guess every now and then exceptions can be made. I didn't want the room to be lit just yet. "Hello darkness my old friend," I sang in a whisper-like voice and closed my eyes, wanting to fall asleep again, but I couldn't. The door abruptly opened and in walked one of the last two people I wanted to see at the moment, Kate.

The sudden flash of light blinded me. My eyes struggled to open, and even when they did manage to do so, it was all very blurry and frustrating but that was the least of my worries. I was drunk and unstable. Soon the hangover will arrive if it hasn't already. This was not the state I planned to confront her in.

The pictures and the envelope were right in front of me in the living room but she couldn't see them as she didn't come to where I sat, she barely even glanced at me. She hurried for the bathroom, frantically turning on every light on her way.

Kate didn't even bother to check if someone was already inside. I used the opportunity to put the pictures back inside the envelope and put it in my pocket, so she couldn't see what it contained, not just yet at least. I took out the pieces off my foot and tried to stand on it. It hurt and I sat back down.

As my eyes adjusted to the bright lights, my mind jumped around, from the alcohol to the door. She just stormed in and went straight to the toilet. Usually she would just turn on the lights that were mostly used. This time she frantically turned on almost all of them. She must've been holding it in for a while. That was very unlike her.

I got up and rather than confronting her outside the bathroom, which was right next to our bedroom. The room where so many great memories had been made, I instead walked to the kitchen. The room where all the knives were kept. I sat on my chair, no longer able to walk as my foot was killing me. *I don't remember jumping on the table.* Not important, I decided. The only thing left for me to do was to wait for her to eventually show up.

As I waited, I noticed that Kate had taken her purse with her in a hurry. Otherwise she would usually put it on the kitchen table. Instead I put the empty bottle of whiskey where her purse used to be.

My senses were still a mess and my head was throbbing with pain but fuck all that. I had questions and complaints and she needed to answer them. It took her several minutes to get back, which gave me more time to prepare myself.

I sat there looking at the empty bottle, wondering if I should use it to demonstrate how I felt. I could hear her walking close by, and I imagined myself throwing the bottle at her, or at least near her, catching her off guard and scaring her. Then I'll finally start with the much awaited Q&A.

Kate finally saw me, and jumped. Her purse in her hand, just zipping it shut. She was still wearing her office clothes and high pencil heels. For some reason she hadn't changed them. She planned on going out again. The look on her face indicated some sort of urgency.

"Didn't see you there," she gasped and let out a small chuckle. She probably didn't see the diamond ring I put on her finger when she was sucking her lover's cock either. "Sorry! I've got a lot in my mind so I somehow didn't even see you," she said again as if I hadn't heard her the first time. I didn't respond to it. I only stared at her.

My eyes struggled to look at her in detail, but it was good, that way I didn't get distracted by the face I fell in love with, the haziness turned out to be a blessing in disguise. My muscle memory however, out of nowhere, decided to hold onto the empty bottle again.

I gripped it tightly between my fingers and her smile faded away as it finally dawned upon her that something was wrong. Whatever her plans were, they were going to get canceled for sure.

"I've been waiting for you," I said, licking my dry lips and wiping the excess saliva on my sleeve.

"Is everything okay, Dave?" she asked, her voice already hinting a sense of panic as she breathes in short successions.

"Doesn't everything look okay?" I said, my grip tightening on the neck of the bottle. I wanted to throw it at her.

"You're drunk. You haven't had a drink in… You quit, remember? Wha- what happened?" she asked, her tone worried. If only she was this thoughtful when she cheated on me.

"Oh, I forgot about that," I said, forcing out a smile.

"You forgot?" she murmured. She paused for a minute, examining me, analyzing and then added, "Should I be worried?"

"I don't know, should you?" I retorted.

"Honey, you're freaking me out," she stepped back, afraid. She might run away. I didn't want her to leave just yet. Her friends can wait, they'll have to.

"Oh, I'm sorry, sweetheart, it's just… the week, this week has been a total nightmare," she's quiet, that's good. "You know I actually suspected you," the words came out of my mouth so easily, it was as if I was not the one even saying them. It was almost like watching a movie and listening to a character from that movie say things in a rushed tone.

"Suspected me? Of what?" she frowned. *Take a guess bitch.* "What are you talking about?"

"I'm talking about you fucking someone who is not your husband," I searched my pockets for the envelope and found it just seconds later.

Her face now had more clarity to it. Her eyes met mine. She was shocked and it felt great to let it all out. I kept my eyes on her as I opened the envelope and raised it up, like cheers. I didn't take out the pictures completely, just a small part of it. I raised it and let her guess what it was?

"What's that?" she asked, but something in her tone told me, she already knew, or at least suspected.

"The proof of your unfaithfulness," Her eyes looked away from me and instead at the envelope, then her head bowed down, *defeated*. She was no longer going to hide it, it seemed. *That was quick.*

"Oh my God, you're bleeding," she pointed at my foot.

"Don't change the fucking subject." I yelled. She jumped as if I just electrocuted her.

We stayed there for a while, neither one of us saying a word. I let the awkward silence fill up the room for as long as I could. With each passing second, she was getting more and more uncomfortable and I knew she would be the one to break the silence. I was right.

"I… I'm not sure if I understand what you mean," she whispered, playing dumb. I could hear it but I pretended not to. I threw the envelope at her. I expected her to catch it but she didn't. Instead it slapped her across her chest and fell to the floor, near her feet. Some of the pictures fell out.

The picture of her on her knees was the last one I remembered putting in the envelope so it had to be the first one to fall out. "I'm sorry," she whispered again, this time loud enough for her to know that I could hear her, that I could hear her sobs through her words. I could but it wasn't enough.

"I… I'm not sure what I should ask you first, if anything. I'm not sure if I should discuss this with you or… maybe with a lawyer. I may also need a banker to loan me some change for the therapy I'm going to need after this. Is there someone good you would recommend for me? You're the one with all the contacts, are you not?"

"How…" she let out a whimper, still not looking at me. "How did you find out?" she asked, in a high pitched crybaby voice. God I love the change in her voice. Despite the circumstances I couldn't help but find it cute.

"Does it matter? Will that change the fact that my lovely wife…" I said it as if I was announcing it. "Was out there fucking some hot shot banker, while I'm told she's busy with work?" She looked at me with wide eyes, shocked, as she should've been from the very beginning, better late than never. The first week of our marriage I had kissed those huge eyes of hers, Anime eyes I used to call it. It had tickled her yet I kept doing it. Now I wanted to stab them, bite them in half and watch them bleed.

She broke eye contact and bent forward. Her hand reached for the envelope and the pictures that had fallen out. I put the empty bottle back on the table as she pulled out the rest of the pictures. She froze where she stood as she went through them one by one. She took her time staring at them and examining them, to the point she'd probably seen the pictures in more detail than I ever did. I left her to it, hoping, expecting her to break down crying as she skims all of them over and over again.

"Have you seen all of these?" she asked. I sat straighter in my chair.

That was not at all the question I was expecting her to ask. I tried my best to hide my surprise but it wasn't good enough. She can read me like a book at this point of our marriage and knowing her, so could I.

Something was wrong. She wasn't just looking at the pictures anymore, she was picking them. She took a handful and put them in her purse. Then she put back the rest of them in the envelope.

"I'm sorry you had to find out like this," she threw the envelope back at me and I quickly picked it up. "It was a mistake but I'm glad you found out. I can't live with this anymore," I tore off the packet like an animal. The pictures weren't that clear but I could still tell that they all only consisted of her and the banker.

The one with the motel was gone, so were some of the ones with her other friends and colleagues. The pictures got fuzzier as my head started to get heavy. I was still somewhat drunk and for a second I felt like I was going to fall down, yet I forced myself up with the strength I forgot I ever had.

One of the ways I did this was by forcing my brain to realize what just happened. "I'm sorry you had to find out the way you did."

"It wasn't the banker, was it?" I said, finally realizing what just happened, angered at the fact that I just paid for the wrong evidence, yet still caught the right criminal. If it were the banker there wouldn't be a need to remove the rest.

Her silence gave me my answers, along with the slight head tilt she does whenever she's ashamed of something. I knew I was right. "Who was it then?" I spoke through clenched teeth and it took everything I had not to straight up scream the question at her.

"No one you need to know," Her hand started fidgeting inside her bag. *Nervous?* "Have you seen all of the pictures?" I had, but I didn't tell her, I couldn't speak. *Shit! How could I be so stupid?* I had seen all of them but I only focused on the banker. I had seen some others but I couldn't remember any of them anymore as I just brushed them off as unimportant.

She kept one of her hands inside her purse as the other one held it from outside. All the while glancing at both me and the purse simultaneously. She was doing something to the photos, crumpling them? Tearing them apart? Nah, she'll struggle to tear them even if she used both hands, let alone inside a handbag. Whatever it was that she was doing, I knew it couldn't be good. The ones she'd kept, probably had the cheater in them.

I stood up and started to walk towards her, it was hard to balance myself but I managed, even if for a while. I tried to hide the pain I felt. I needed to find out who he was. She won't tell me that easily. I know that much about her, she's a tough girl. *I might have to knock the answer out of her, and at this point I might as well will.* There was no going back.

Five

"Give it back," I demanded, barely able to walk straight but far from caring. I shouldn't have drunk the entire bottle and I shouldn't have broken the table either. She's never going to tell me which ones I'm looking for, so here was my chance, as risky as it was. I had to take it from her. I had to force my way to the answers I wanted. The answers she owed me.

"There's no need for that," Kate held up a hand at me, signaling me to stay back, and the hell I would. "I'm glad you found out. I've been meaning to confess," her breathing was quick, yet the tone was harsh and rowdy. She didn't stop me by using force, but by words, the way she usually would. Before she even finished her next sentence, I knew, I won't like where this was gonna go. "I can't take this anymore. I think we should see other people."

See other people? Are you fucking kidding me? "You're joking right? This isn't your high school, teenage b-boyfriend, girlfriend thing going on. We're fucking married," talking was hard, the words came out a jumbled mess yet I couldn't stop myself. "We shared our vows and had everyone witness it like the event it was. Your parents, our friends and relatives, all of them saw us become a family of our own..." My voice broke. I wanted to keep ranting but stopped, not sure if I could carry on any longer. There was so much I had in mind to tell, to explain to her, to remind her how our marriage was not a game or a stupid fling but that it's one of the best things that ever happened to me in my shitty life. But the more I came close to letting out how I honestly felt the more broken I felt. I stopped talking. If living those moments with me didn't stop her, what made me think my monologue would?

"Look, I know how you feel. I…" I shut her off after that. I didn't want her to tell me any more lies. I don't think I have enough patience to sit through her trying to justify it.

"You don't know shit. I loved you and you betrayed me. Every day I kept wishing I was wrong. Every time you said you love me these past few days, I had to pretend I believed you. I had to pretend I was the only one you said it to, the only one you at least meant it to," my voice broke again, this time to the point my words mixed up in an unintelligible way and I had to pause to wipe my sniffling nose.

In front of her stood a grown man weeping like a young boy whose favorite balloon just got popped by a bully. As I wiped off my snot with my hand, I felt a small scratch under my nose. It was the ring. I stared at my now meaningless wedding ring as the minister's voice echoed in my head. *You may exchange the rings. I now pronounce you man and wife. You may kiss the bride.* Only in my head it was 'kill' instead of kiss.

"Don't insult me by lying to me," I said in a much calmer way, a bargaining tone. "You know fully well you don't know how I feel. If you did, you wouldn't have gone through with it the first time. Especially after what I told you about my family, when I trusted you and told you about my mother and what she did. How it ruined my family forever," Mentioning my mother brought back some of the rage and a lot of pain.

Maybe this is Karma. I had failed then and so I was getting punished now. Except I was nowhere near as bad as dad. Then again, that wasn't a fair comparison. If you're a better person than Hitler, does that automatically make you a good person?

"I'm sorry, I… I didn't mean for it to happen," she swallowed and now she had both her hands in front of her, in front of us. I could see the small shiny ring on her finger. All those months I spent choosing between the designs, and the savings I had to spend on it. *To go through all of that, just to come to this.* "I think we should talk about this some other time. When you're… better," no, NO. You're not going to get away from me like that.

I might be drunk but not stupid. Even in a shit state like this, I could make out the image of her hands and skinny fingers. The ones she pulled out from her purse. Her fingers were painted red, but it wasn't blood. It looked like lipstick and smelled like, like nail polish.

"So it wasn't the banker, but then it must be one of the lawyers you work with, or maybe your boss. Did he promise you a raise?" Imagining her like that, like a secretary seducing her boss for a promotion made my lips twitch into a grin. "You've always enjoyed some foreplay," she shook her head, rejecting the notion but I'm not convinced. Maybe it was the thrill she got fucking the other guy that made her this way. "Did he also promote your friend's carriers? An orgy full of Lawyers will be quite a sight I'll admit."

"Life is more complicated than that," she said in her "we're *not kids anymore*" tone. The tone she used whenever she thought I was being immature. Then she put her red hand back into the bag. She was back to scribbling all over the photos again. I was done stalling, it was time to act, but how? I have to think of a better way, a less violent way if I can.

"Sure it is. I would know. Wouldn't I?" she closed her purse as I took my first step in her direction and hid it behind her. The window of opportunity for me to snatch it had left, for now. I took far too long to make a move. I should've known she had to be taking in the possibilities of me forcing the photos. She may have even considered my foot as a liability and she was right. No matter how much I ignored it, it still hurt like hell. If she started running, I would've lost. Right now the best option was to gain some more energy first. Let the foot rest a little, just for now.

"He was introduced by an old friend. Just moved to the states and..." She took a deep breath. "Things happened so fast..."

"Spare me the details of how he was so handsome and you were so horny, that you forgot you had a husband at home," I said as I sat back on my chair, my head hurt, body spineless and all emotions exhausted. I just wanted to lie down somewhere, preferably on the street during busy traffic.

"It's not like that and you know it," her voice louder than earlier. "It's more complicated than that. You were always busy at work, we both were. I felt like a machine more than a human," *what a fucking cliché of an answer? Come on darling, you can do better than that.* The words lined up in my mouth, but struggled to come out.

"So that's why you did it? Because it made you feel like a human? Did fucking me make you feel like a fucking bot?"

"Yes," her quick response made me flinch. I tried to quickly hide it with a laugh. "Laugh all you want, but deep down you know we were both just going by the day like soulless slaves. I'm actually glad you found out. Now we can move on from our lives," Kate's words killed my fake laughter as soon as it had come.

"Move on? Wait what? So you don't want to talk it through, or fix our marriage?" *what the fuck is wrong with you?* You are supposed to apologize and then we would try and find a way to make it work, to fix this mess and in turn, our lives. But you've already given up on me, on us. *Is this really it for us?*

"There's no need for that. I think it's better if we just went our separate ways. It's not like it's too late or something. We're still young enough and we don't have any children either. We should just split and there won't be any trouble. You can go your way and I'll go mine. We could still choose a better path for our lives," *I don't like this.* Her tone has changed. It's more a matter of fact now. She is way past just thinking about it. She has already decided on it, whether I was all in for it or not. She's just here to explain the terms to me. "You can find someone better than me…" This time I shook my head, a little too hard for my state and it hurt.

"I don't want someone better than you. I want you," that shut her up, for now. "I want you and me to stay the way we are. This is just a bump we hit. All marriages stumble into issues eventually but that doesn't mean we quit. I still love you Goddamn it," I said and meant it. I always loved her. My entire angry, tough persona was gone. I might as well be begging in front of her, as if I was the one who was caught cheating on her.

"But I don't," the way she said it, so… so easily. *How can you say that Kate?* "I… I don't mean it like that. I just want us to be friends at best. I really think we should just seek a different life," She was no longer the person I knew.

"Did I do something unforgivable?" I plead. I thought of what could've possibly happened between us that drove her to this. I never hit her or embarrassed her in public. I've rarely, if ever, called her any nasty words. I even tried my best to cheer her up during the miscarriage. I looked at her again but I didn't see the woman who said, 'I do' at the altar, not anymore.

"It's not you it's me," Another cliché line. The Kate I knew was way more original than that. It was like she changed into a stranger that I was meeting for the first time. Someone who just pretended to be nice, to be my friend but clearly wasn't interested in me or my life. "You're a good person," I couldn't take it anymore. Her lies, her words, time to stop them both.

"Give me the pictures," I stiffened my fist and took a giant step forward. My mind and body were both overwhelmed with all the shit they had just been through. I no longer felt hesitant that I might have to use force on her, and at that point, a part of me even wanted to. The way she kept shaking her head just pissed me off. I hated her deciding what was best for me, for her, for us. I was not going to let her tell me what to do any more. I wanted to, hell I needed to see that man. *Was it the blonde?*

"There is no need for that," she hid the purse behind her again, like earlier, but it wasn't enough to stop me this time. Even the bleeding foot wasn't going to stop me. I'd chase her down even if I had just one leg.

"I'll be the judge of that," My own voice sounded alien to me. Someone else was speaking from my mouth, just like how somebody else was in charge of my body. I was full of this animalistic energy that I hadn't felt in years, and it took some effort to keep it under control, to not let it control me.

"Stop it!" she hesitated but it was too late. I forced the purse out of her grip, a broken fingernail fell on the floor as I ripped it open. She scratched my hand and I had to let go. I managed to seize some photos and went through them as blood dripped from my hand. As expected, she had scribbled all the faces on the pictures with her nail polish. I could barely make out anything but there was still a lead.

"It was the blonde, wasn't it?" she had covered half of his entire face, or at least the side of the face. I tried to rub it out but it just worsened. Fuck! The bitch was smart and it kept rubbing me the wrong way. But no worries, all I had to do was just call the guy again and get the pictures back, this time of the right person. *I got him.* But wait, there was another picture of a different colleague and she'd covered his face too. "Fuck! This is a trick," That way I couldn't tell which one he really was. Any of these could be him. I've reached my boiling point.

"It's for the best. This way…" she started to speak and what stopped her from finishing her sentence was my fist. All the pent up rage was in control of my body and just like me, it didn't take too kindly to her judging what I wanted or needed to know either. The wrath I had held in for so long was all out on the surface. Rage took charge, and I let it.

My hand swung towards her, as if acting on its own. It grew faster until it connected with her cheek. All the while my mind forced my lips to ask her who he was. My body however was much faster to react than my words.

Her wide eyes stared back at me as if she genuinely believed she hadn't done anything wrong. That I was punishing her just for the sake of it. She was surprised to see that I was capable of hitting her. I was surprised too. Surprised I didn't do it sooner. This was the first time I'd ever raised my hand on her and unless she gave me what I wanted, this was far from being the last. "Tell me his name," I roared and she stumbled backwards.

"I… I can't," she stuttered as tears came down her cheeks. It was hard to continue, to watch her cry, to control my emotions. Please don't make me do this love.

"You're not going anywhere until you tell me," My pace quickened to hide the pain in my voice. For each step I took, she took two more. The closer I got to her, the further she tried to get away from me. It didn't help her that her steps were a fraction of mine. Even with the way I was walking. No matter how hard she tried, I tried harder. If she walks away, I'll run after her. If she slaps me, I'll punch her. If she scratches my hand, I'll stab hers.

"Please… think about what you're doing?" Kate warned.

"Oh I think we're way past that. You should've thought of that when you cheated on me," I kept reminding myself of what she'd done, to help me feel justified for what I was doing, for the monster I was becoming.

"Assault against a partner is improper," *Is she seriously about to lecture me through her law degree?* I always knew how much she loved showing off even when she wasn't that good at it but this was too much. I wondered if her lover was also obsessed with the law. "It's domestic violence and punishable by…" I grabbed her stuttering little mouth, and shoved her head on the wall behind her.

The impact of her skull on the concrete wall made a thud. A sense of déjà vu hit me and I froze. Dad did a similar thing to mom. I shook the memory off but sadly the reality forced it to stay put. Dad had grabbed mom's head and smashed it against the wall multiple times. I can still recall how her skull bounced off the concrete.

It angered me more and more that this was actually happening. *What did I ever do to deserve this?* I was, I am nothing like dad. I shook off the memory and forced myself to stay in the present.

I looked at Kate, who shivered as if the temperature in the room just dropped arctic. *What did I ever do to you Kate?* I wanted to ask but the words that came out of my mouth were completely different.

"I'll kill you if I have to," I almost spit on her. "Give me his name," Despite my efforts, she barely talked. She instead hit the side of my face with a table lamp and ran towards the kitchen. I heard dad's voice in my head as the words escaped my mouth, "You can't run from me you fucking whore!"

"Stay away from me," She tried to defend herself with the kitchen knife. Her body tried its bravest to fight while her voice begged me to stay back. "Please, I don't want to hurt you," *I wish I could believe that.*

"It's too late for that," I said, each word dipped in hate. I couldn't believe I ever loved this bitch. Her lovely face that I could once stare at for hours, now burned my eyes, even though I could barely see parts of it as tears filled them up, *or is it the lamp she threw at me, or maybe it's the alcohol. It can't be just the eyes as they're not that weak, are they?* I saw her clearly just a few seconds ago and now it's all a blur again. "That knife isn't going to stop me even if it cuts me," *I actually hoped it did.* I wanted it to cut my throat.

I pictured myself in a scenario where that did happen. I'll lay down on the floor bleeding and dying. Maybe I'll see at least some regret on her face. As I rest my head on her lap and her fingers touch my face, a hint of the woman I knew and loved. I would actually welcome an end like that, over this chaos.

"Please, stay back," her pleas went unheard as I jumped at her, the knife barely missing my eye as I grabbed her arm and twisted it. I seized a handful of her hair in my palm, my fingers gripping it tightly. If I could've I would've ripped it all the way off from her skull.

My body moved faster than my mind as I pushed her pretty little head against the tiled wall, smashing that gorgeous face. Her blood left a mark on the pink tiles. She'd chosen them for our kitchen personally. Kate said before buying them that she had her eyes on them for a while. Well now she had her face on them too.

She struggled and kicked, her heels stabbed me on my already injured bare foot. I forgot she still wore them. The pain forced me to let go of her, but I managed to keep my hold on her arm. "Let me go," She pushed me with the strength I forgot she even had, and I fell with my back on the dinner table. The blood under my foot removed the friction and I landed with extra force.

The force shattered the glass table under all of my weight and I dropped on the floor. The hundreds of small pieces of glass stabbed the back of my neck and some even climbed inside my hair, imprinting them on my scalp. As I moved, they pierced through my thin t-shirt and entered my skin. The sky blue t-shirt was replaced by grim red on my back.

I moved my forearm, only to notice it was covered in glass but that was not where my attention remained. The tip of my ring finger touched something, something hard. It was an empty bottle, just inches away from my reach. I looked back up. Her blurred image was making a run for the door. I wasn't going to let that happen, I couldn't let her leave.

In a desperate move, I reached for the bottle. Somehow I managed to grab it. I heard the turning of the door knob. I can't let her leave. It took all my strength to pick up the bottle and as soon as I did, I threw it at her direction, hoping it'll stop her. A part of me even wished it'll knock her out. A hit on the back of the spine or legs should work in slowing her down.

A literal shot in the dark. I wasn't even sure if it hit her. I couldn't get up to check. I was on the brink of passing out when I told myself I couldn't let that happen. I forced myself up; the tiny pieces of glass helped me from falling back again.

I managed to stand on my knees and saw that my aim, as indistinct as it was, as unreliable as it was, had still managed to hit the target. The empty bottle shattered as it hit her skull. A result, more terrifying than I was expecting.

The impact from the dense bottle on the back of her head pushed her face at the front, causing her to break her nose on the hard edge of the door. Blood exploded from her face and suddenly I got the urge to watch her choke on it. I fought the urge. *'I can't'* I tell myself. I am not like that, I'm not like him. I had to stop myself from not doing anything.

I grabbed her and pulled her off the ground. I made her sit with her back onto the wall. It took a lot of strength to help her sit properly, and even more so to stop myself from bashing her head onto the very wall she was using for support.

I closed the door and locked it before any neighbors showed up although I doubt they will. Not having any nosy neighbors was one of our main priorities during the apartment hunting. *Awful neighbors can make incredible houses feel like prison,* she had once said. *Great inmates make prison feel like home,* I had replied.

The condition of her face was much worse than I wanted. She could barely move and was losing way too much blood. Her gray blouse turned red, from both front and back. If the bleeding wasn't stopped, she would die. A part of me wanted to see her suffer but the rest wanted her to survive. She was still my wife after all. *We can deal with our issues later, when both of us are in a better state,* both physically and mentally. The horrific sight was helping me get hold of my sanity.

I searched for my phone. The Ambulance was what we needed. Her bloodied face was utterly unrecognizable which helped to dissolve my rage almost completely. As much as I hated her, I didn't want her to die, at least not here, not when I would be the obvious main suspect.

"First we'll have to fix that disgusting face of yours," I said, trying to distract her pain with some forced humor, but I doubt she even heard me.

I couldn't find my phone. I thought I may need to drive her there, but could I? I was barely able to walk straight myself. I couldn't even see properly without my glasses. I could see the things near me with at least some clarity but anything a few feet away and it gets worse than a child's water painting. *How the fuck would I drive?*

I looked for her purse and found it. I scattered everything she had in it all over the floor. I finally found her phone but hesitated to dial. Not because of the pictures I found there, even though some of them were cleaner than others and a part of me did want to examine them. I stopped because of something else, something way worse. My mind struggled to make any decisions once I saw it, and as time passed she got worse.

A minute ago, I was worried that she might die if it's too late, but now, I fucking hoped she would. If not I might even go as far as to kill her myself, not out of sympathy, I've lost all of that, but out of rage. Grabbing her by the throat and pushing in harder and harder as blood poured out of her face like a river.

I shook my head, I'm not a killer but I couldn't just forgive her either. So I just stood there. *I'm not going to kill her but I don't have to save her either, not anymore.*

Six

Blood poured out of her now unrecognizable face and onto her clothes, then her stomach, all the way down to her thighs. Her eyes still watched me and only me. They haven't closed for a while. I remember watching movies where when someone dies but has his eyes open, someone else closes them down for him. I didn't trust myself enough to do that to Kate.

In an instant, all the love I had for her in my heart vanished. It was instead replaced with disbelief, and disappointment. I looked down on her soon to be rotting corpse of a body and then at the scattered purse. I couldn't help but stomp on it and everything that came out of it, especially it. I destroyed everything she owned, just for the sake of it, covering all of it with my own blood. The pain from the foot was nothing more than a scratch at this point. *I just killed my wife, does it really matter what else I do after that?*

Once I was done with her bag, I looked back at her. She was still bleeding but this time slower, maybe she ran out of blood, either that or her heart stopped beating completely. Her eyes were as lifeless as her heart. *Have I done the right thing? Or have I overreacted? I don't know, maybe both, maybe neither.*

Several minutes went by as I stood still, thinking what I had just done and especially what I'd have to do next? Do I surrender to the cops or do I dispose of her body? It was an accident, wasn't it? It's not like I aimed for her head. I let out a long noisy breath. It's too late to think about it now. I can't keep her here. I need to get rid of her body, and fast.

I couldn't take her to the hospital anymore as it was pretty clear it wouldn't help. They'll just end up calling the cops, who will then blow it all up to the roof for me. Even more so once they do a background check on me. So the only solution I could think of was to hide her body and figure out the rest as I went.

There was no other option I could come up with. I decided to bury her somewhere. There was a lake half a mile away, up north. I couldn't remember its name but I could still use the GPS to get there, its big enough to be easily found on any map.

If memory serves right, the place was open, and between the woods. People jog there in the morning and some lovebirds stay up till the sunset. So if I went there, it would have to be at night, when it's dark and empty. I had to get there, find a spot and throw her there. *That place is big enough for her to be buried and not be found for decades,* dad's voice came back.

I started calculating the possibilities all over again. There would be a larger risk of getting caught if I threw her in the water, but I'll have to take that. The place had enough stones to tie her to and was deep enough for her body to get lost. Now I knew what I had to do, but *will I be able to go forward with it without being seen or caught?*

I laid face first on the couch in the living room. Same place where I sat when I opened the envelope. My mind was exhausted and my body tired. I once read that even a small nap can help clear up your mind. But then again, I doubt there were any wife killers in the survey. I sat up on the couch, with my knees sinking in the seat and my hands holding my empty head between them. I knew I had to wait for the right time. *But what was the right time? Is there a right time? Can you even google for shit like this?*

The bright stars looked down on me. Their shine burst in the dark sky as I stared out of the window. My body is still and slow while my mind is blank as a board. Mom used to sit me down on the garden grass and tell me that those stars look close, but are very far. *Like dad?* I had asked. She didn't reply. I hate that garden for what dad did there.

I waited for almost an hour before I finally made my move. I waited for it to get safe enough so I could take her out. Until then, I had to prepare. I had to fix it, otherwise I'll just break again.

Like a good househusband, I cleaned the floor and the walls, making them shine almost. Like a respectful gentleman, I covered my lady's wounds so she doesn't bleed anymore and hence doesn't leave any unwanted mess behind, which would be very unladylike of her. I got the first aid kit and used the bandage to cover her busted face up. Good thing I don't need glasses to look at things that are closer to me, or were.

With the center of her face covered, I then proceeded to cover the rest of her with a blanket. The warm thick blanket that we bought for winter, the same one she wore when I got the text yesterday. She had once wrapped me inside it when I was sick. She took care of me when I caught cold last winter and even came early from work. She used to be a fucking angel. Maybe she still was. Maybe I was the monster who cut off her wings. What the fuck have I done? *No. no... Stop thinking about it.* She deserved it and that's that or… *But Did she?* Whichever the case, I had to change the blanket I was using.

I looked for something to tie her up with. We didn't own any ropes. We never had any use for it. I only had a jump rope that I could think of to use. Then I remembered that I had already lost it during a walk. I'd accidentally forgotten it at the park bench weeks ago. It was time for DIY. So I used my ties and belts.

I cleaned the kitchen from the mess she created. The broken glass that I forgot was still buried on my back, and several pieces of it are still on the kitchen floor. Luckily almost all the glass pieces came out of my back once I pulled out the t-shirt. The shower took care of the rest. The blood on the wall and the one on the floor were gone but some stains remained. I decided to clean the rest of her blood later. For now, I had to take care of her.

I put her on the couch, this way I only saw her when I needed to. It was dark but not dark enough to move out, begging the question, how much darker do I want it to get. I needed half an hour more at least, I decided. To kill some more time, I hid the broken tables away and wrapped my foot with bandages, along with the back. But I still had time left and I couldn't afford to pause. Every time I stopped doing something, I started to think of her.

Every item we owned or bought together reminded me of us, of her, of the memories I didn't need reminded, not now not ever. From the bookshelf to the paintings, all the way to the answering machine, especially the answering machine. She was the one who bought it, despite me constantly reminding her that phones exist and are better.

Kate had won that argument regardless of my logic, by simply stating that her parents used to own an older model when she was a kid. *How do you counter that?* Answer, *you can't. Nostalgia is a bitch.* She got a newer model but then paid extra to have an older design. She even recorded her voice the very hour it arrived and adjusted its setting for maximum recording limit.

You've reached Dave and Kate, we may be busy at the moment, so please feel free to leave a message right after the beep, thank you for calling. It took her seventeen tries to get that. I'm just glad she settled for a quick sentence and didn't actually go for the limit. Otherwise she would've spent the whole day with it.

I was tempted to listen to it, to hear her voice again. Now that I knew I won't get to hear it, I missed it even more. I shook the feeling away. *I can always do it later, not that I even want to. I might as well just break the damn thing.*

I searched under the pillows, in the bathroom cupboard and finally found it in the drawer. *My old glasses.* I rarely used them. My hands trembled as I put them on and even though they were old, outdated and slightly cracked; I could still see things with more clarity with it than without.

I walked around the room, unable to stay still. *What else is there for me to do? I've cleaned, moved, organized everything yet I don't feel tired.* I still had enough energy to run a marathon. I went to the bathroom and prepared myself to masturbate, hoping it'll drain at least some of the adrenaline. I pictured what usually turned me on, but that I soon realized was a mistake.

There are moments in my life that play inside my head like a theater when I close my eyes and think about them. When I'm sad, I think of the time Kate and I went on our honeymoon to France. When I'm angry, I think of the time we went to the UK for our anniversary. When I'm scared, I think of when I almost signed up to run in front of the bulls in Spain. Kate talked me out of it, I bet she regrets it now.

I pulled up the toilet seat and brought my pants down to my knees. I was as flaccid as a sock and was not even remotely in the mood, yet I started rubbing it. At first I thought of the memory that usually turns me on instantly. For our anniversary, Kate decided to go into one of those empty red phone booths and call in a special number.

I pictured the moment as well as I could, to the best of my abilities. Kate, on her knees and my dick as hard as a rock. There were 3, maybe 4 of those booths lined up together and it was dark. From her licking the tip to choking on it, all the way to swallowing. It took just 3 minutes for us to be done, which was great because I heard some footsteps coming towards us as we left. Neither of us turned back.

That's one of the things I loved about her and usually it's enough to get me off but not this time. When she smiled I didn't see her warm pink cheeks, instead I saw a bloodied, beaten up face looking back at me with torn up lips. Blood dripped down from her nose and jaw. Needless to say, it ruined the whole moment.

I searched my mind for a different memory but I couldn't find it. Not because I couldn't think of them. Kate is, or… was, the embodiment of crazy fun. A strict lawyer from outside and a pure degenerate from the inside. She had the guts to challenge me into doing things I wouldn't dream to do and she would always bring out the best of me. Her memories weren't the issue. It was her damaged face that appeared in all of them. Every time I looked back on all the fond memories with Kate, all of them had her with a broken nose, even the bad ones. *I can't go on like this.* I pulled my pants back up again.

"Fuck it!" I struck my head on the bathroom wall and walked out, defeated. Another look at Kate's corpse and I decided my next move. The more time I spend waiting for the right time, the harder it gets to go through with it. So now, no more waiting. *I have to get rid of her. I can't just keep stalling anymore.*

I wasn't able to shake off the feeling that things were going to get worse. I needed to prepare for the worst. If things do go worse than they already have, I'd need all the help I could get. I've never wanted to do this but I had no choice. If I'm caught, I'll need him to be there.

I prepared a text for uncle cliff. He's a high profile lawyer and I hoped I wouldn't need him. I saved the text to draft, a last minute resort. I made sure my location was on for him to trace me. I did not want him to be involved in the slightest, but it wouldn't hurt to have a backup plan. I had to listen to my brain and not my emotions', listening to emotions was what got me into this trouble in the first place.

I peeked outside the window. *No one's there.* Then I opened my door ever so slightly to see if there was anyone in the hallway, no one there either. With adrenaline pumping through my veins like a drug and sweat practically covering my entire forehead, I picked her up and headed for the elevator. She wasn't as heavy as I remembered.

I put her on the floor as we went down. The top of her scalp was visible and I stared at the line in the middle, where I used to rub oil in. She loved the way I massaged her head. I hated hers. Her nails were like knives. At times it felt like she was typing a report on my skull. When I complained about it, she just laughed it off. I was going to miss that smile as well.

The doors opened and I hurried to pick her up, memories can wait, if not downright disappear. The car was only meters away and there was no one at the parking lot either. Either that or my mind was just showing me what I wanted to see. I had not yet fully recovered from the drink or the rest.

The glasses didn't help much either as they struggled to balance on my nose. It was broken at one point and I'd done a terrible job fixing it. I should've just gotten contacts, like Kate had suggested. Instead I opted for the easier option, even though I kept forgetting where I put them half the time.

Regardless I put her body on the backseat of the car for the time being. I walked to the back to open the trunk but before I could open it, I heard something. A noise, I listened closely, it was a horn. A car was approaching and would soon get to where I stood in seconds.

I couldn't afford to be seen, so I ditched the trunk and pushed her body all the way in. I closed the doors, and then got in myself. I could hear the car get closer and started the engine. I felt like a superhuman doing it at the pace I was. I checked back and Kate might as well just be sleeping behind me, inside a sleeping bag of course.

The car entered and it was a Scorpio. Big car with a higher window. I kicked in the pedals and drove past it rapidly to avoid getting seen, or so I thought. I don't think the driver saw me, at least I hoped he didn't. But I noticed him looking in my direction. He was an older man, the type who wore sunglasses at night to look cool. Probably just returned from some party. When I was checking on him through the glass, my heart sank. I forgot to close the window on the back seat.

With deep breaths that pushed my lungs to their limit, I drove out the gate and straight onto the main street. Soon I'll be on the main road. *This might have been a mistake. What if the driver of that car recognized my car and then me? What is going to be my alibi? Maybe I'll have to get rid of this car as well and if asked, say Kate was the one who drove it. Will that even work? Will I come across convincing or like an idiot?*

It was dark outside. The street lights were helpful but only a little. More and more cars surrounded me as I got closer to my destination. The street was far from being clear but I could still make out the image of cars driving near me well enough and there were a lot, way too many for me to handle. *I should've taken more rest before I headed out.*

It was dim and my eyes weren't that trustworthy. I cursed myself for drinking as much as I had and wanted to rip these eyes off my head, along with my brain as it was also getting useless. I couldn't even concentrate on anything. Add to that, I forgot to refill the fuel in my car.

I took a deep breath and counted to ten. *I can deal with these irritations later.* I just needed to make sure I didn't get caught. "Deep breath," I told myself, over and over again as I tried not to rub my eyes or hold my head.

Just get rid of her and then be done with it, start a new life or something, probably never get married again. *I can't stay, can I?* I'd have to sell the apartment and leave for tomorrow as soon as possible. A different city... *fuck, this is all so stupid. I should just go to the cops and confess about everything.*

I almost turned the car around. *No wait, I... I can't.* Then everyone would know, and then HE will know. Everyone will talk about it. What should I do? "Fuck. FUCK. FUCK!" I Scream. If only I could get a guarantee that he won't find out then I'll happily surrender. Just thinking of him knowing and then mocking me, makes my blood boil.

He would surely enjoy that. Dad loves reminding me of my fuck ups.

Kate already smelled awful behind me. A dead body isn't supposed to stink this soon. Maybe she just released her bowls or something. First my heart, then my eyes, then my head and now even my nose was getting assaulted. "It's your entire fault Kate," I take a quick turn to the left, better safe than sorry. I headed for the tunnel.

The tunnel was not a shortcut but a longer one which made it ideal for me as it meant the road would be far less populated, if not straight up abandoned, which would be even better. As expected, it was empty, no one used it. Some kids used to race here, before an accident stopped it.

At night, during time like this, it was even scarier to be around. Since people stopped using this route, it hadn't been that well maintained or protected. People could get mugged here, or killed, or on the opposite side, you could shoot a porno here with the stars groaning and moaning out loud.

The tunnel was also extremely old and rough. Add to that, the fact that most of the lights on the other half did not even work well and you have yourselves the perfect accident prone street. I could accidentally run over homeless people sleeping on the street, or crash a horny couple's party. So I made sure I drove in the dead center.

I'd just have to be careful of other cars, trucks and especially cops, just in case they were around. I also had to make sure that there weren't any dumb teenagers around, pulling off stupid stunts on their dad's bikes.

Thankfully there was no one for a distance. In no time, I approached the dark area but it also meant if someone approached me, I'd see them use the lights or maybe a horn. Maybe it was because I was tired and drunk or maybe because I'd been sleeping at exactly this time of the day on a regular basis for years without missing a beat, but whatever it was, was a nightmare.

As the darkness covered me like an icy blanket, I struggled to keep my eyes open. I couldn't understand how despite going through all this shit, my mind was still not done with me. My head was throbbing, making my eyelids heavy. Usually there's light at the end of the tunnel but in this case, in my case, there was nothing but darkness. My head started to spin and I felt dizzy.

I slowed down my car, but not by much as I started losing control of everything. I had to make sure I didn't crash on the walls. I take my right hand off the steering wheel and slap myself, yelling "Wake the fuck up!" I wasn't careful enough. I slowed down and drove as carefully as I could but it was no use. I kept my lights on but took far too long to see it coming. No matter how hard I tried, Shit still ended up hitting the fan.

As my grip tightened around the steering wheel and I barely missed a fatal concussion on the head, thanks to the seatbelt. My eyes adjusted and I realized, I'd just hit a car.

The impact could've been worse if I hadn't slowed down but it also would've been avoided if my eyes hadn't decided on being lazy at the last second. *It doesn't matter. It's too late to complain about it.* I searched for my glasses and found what remained of it over the steering wheel. I put them on and witnessed the rest of the nightmare in more quality.

The non-driver's side, in front of my car, was squashed in like a punctured football and my whole body hurt. I turned the key and the way my car sounded, it was as if the engine was halfway out of its shell. I looked at the black and white car that was just parked there. It was on the side of the road, but somewhat closer to the middle for some reason, and it was big enough to be a van, yet without any lights on. Or maybe I didn't see it and the crash broke its lights too. *It may not be invisible but who the fuck parks like that?*

What made it worse is that I could've easily avoided it and drove from the side if I weren't so bloody distracted. If only I could've managed to get a grip on myself. *It's my fault. It's always my fault.* Maybe this was just something they did to make sure no one was speeding, or racing. Regardless I couldn't stay. I started the car again but it only made noise. It couldn't pull back. That was when the car lit up and a shadow moved inside. *Is someone sleeping there? Did a fucking homeless man park there?*

Then it got worse. There was more than one person in the car, moving and cursing. I didn't dare walk out of my car to check on them. Instead I pulled up the cracked window. It only came halfway up. I locked the door, I have no idea if it worked. I couldn't afford to get seen but the fucking car just wouldn't start. My back hurt as the seat I sat on shifted from the impact and their car windows were high so I couldn't even properly look at them, not that I wanted to. 'This day can't possibly get any worse', I muttered but I was proven wrong almost immediately.

I began to cry. I wanted to leave. I could barely see anything anymore. It was terrifying. My heart was beating in my mouth. They were going to call someone. They'd find Kate. I tried to reverse, to escape, my knuckles turning white on the steering wheel. I strained and pulled, and the damn wheel broke off. My shaking hands failed to slow it down as it hit me in my mouth. I was stuck in my seat and couldn't even move. My mouth was covered in blood.

The car that I hit then started to shine colors and made a very familiar noise. The colors were red and blue and the noise was a siren. It dawned upon me that I had just hit a cop car. *I just can't catch a break, can I? Just my fucking luck.* I couldn't control myself and I burst out laughing like a wild animal, hitting my head with the detached steering wheel, punching the car and wailing, snot ran down my nose, along with blood. I tasted both of them.

"WHAT FUCKING LUCK I HAVE?" I screamed and laughed at the same time. Spit flies out of my busted lips along with drops of blood. The first time I ever killed someone, I went straight to the cops myself. What an obedient criminal I am? The cops got out of their car, stretching, shrugging off the impact as if they just came off a fall on the playground and not a car crash. One of them was tall enough to be a basketball player. Even if I somehow managed to run, he'd catch me in seconds.

"Damn, this was a pretty big one," the shorter one said.

"Lighten up, It's not like you have to pay for the damage," the tall one said.

"I know that, but that doesn't mean we're crash proof. One of these days, it may get fatal," *if only it was this time.*

"Stop whining, this is the first time someone hit this hard. Asshole must be really drunk," *that's true, I'm an asshole and I happen to be drunk.*

"I'm just saying. Next time, let's just leave the car here or maybe some barricade and sit back to catch the crazy kids from a distance," *how about a crazy wife murderer? Two for the price of one.*

"Why? So we can have a hit and miss and not even know who did it? Do you see how dark this place is," *If only I was that lucky, or smart.*

"I get that but how often is it a hit like this? Most punks just leave a bump at best and it's not like we're able to find them all the time. Kids these days are sharp," the other one ignored him as he looked at the back of their car.

"This guy better be alive," *I'd rather not.* His tone was surprisingly casual. It was as if he was watching all this happen on TV or something. They each came at me separately from the sides, holding a torch and it doesn't take a rocket scientist to understand that I'm trapped. If you have a halfway decent nose you'd even catch the stench of alcohol coming off me.

"What do we have here?" one of the cops said, flashing the torch right at my face. *A loser.*

"Another reckless driver, that's what. God the smell alone this shit's giving," *I'm sorry I forgot to take a long proper bath earlier today. I'm pretty sure even your asshole smells better than I do.*

"Hey jackass, thought you can still speed up here? Look at you, all beat up like a ragdoll. Bet you didn't see us. We're always waiting around for idiots like you to…"

"Fuck!" the short one cussed, interrupting the tall one. He flashed the torch behind me, where Kate was. I looked at the back seat, surprisingly able to move that much, and so did the other guy.

"What happened? He's a druggy too?" he seemed to be enjoying this. *Yes I am, alcohol counts as a drug right?*

"Much worse."

I glanced over my shoulder at Kate. The crash had unraveled her. The blanket hiding my crime had fallen to the floor. Her face was hardly visible in the dark, but anyone with a brain could look at the sight and tell, "There's a dead body in the car," I just smiled and laughed, and cried all at the same fucking time as the cops called their headquarters.

The tall one tried to pull the door open but struggled. I never wanted to do this again, I thought those days were done, but I had no choice left. I took out my phone and managed to send the text I had saved earlier. Somehow my phone survived the crash. I clicked send, with fingers that didn't shake this time somehow, just in time for the cop to rip off the car door. I put the phone back in my pocket as the officer grabbed me. The seatbelts were torn off so I was jerked out of it. I no longer had the will to stand and so I fell down, hugging the ground immediately. I expected him to pick me up but he didn't. He instead put his knee on me and cuffed my hands behind me.

"You have the right to remain silent…." The short cop kept talking but I didn't listen. My mind instead shifted its attention elsewhere. Everything happened so fast that I couldn't or maybe I just didn't want to pay attention to anything anymore.

There was a track of ants underneath my cheeks, marching and tickling me. I could smell them and as some of them entered my mouth, I even tasted them. Some just climbed on my chin and I let them. If anything I preferred their company more. I pictured them eating me alive like in those nature documentaries.

I closed my eyes, chuckled a bit as it tickled more and more and hoped to pass out by the time I would evidently be put behind bars.

Seven

The next things that happened, happened so fast that it honestly felt like a quick montage of events in a TV show rather than in real life, and not even a good TV show at that but a lazily written one. It's like when you watch a movie but can only recall certain scenes when you come out of the theater.

The cops arrested me, that's a given. I'm put in a cell where I was left to rot until I woke up hours later. During my hangover, Uncle Cliff shows up with his good old black leather briefcase, a new Rolex and the same old *toupee*? I guess some things never change. We had a little chat inside a room with some privacy that he managed for us to get. I confessed to most of what I'd done. He heard half of it then shook his head and told me what 'really' happened.

I'm supposed to be the victim after all, *right*? Uncle tells me this new improved reality. She cheated on me, things got heated, we had a little 'accident', I was trying to help her by taking her to the nearby hospital and that was when the cops caught me. Good thing there was an actual hospital nearby, *only several kilometers away.* I was in mental and physical distress as can be proven through blood tests, the two cops whose car I rear ended and the CCTV camera at my building's elevator which caught me bringing a bottle and an envelope with me. From finding out about her infidelity to being drunk as hell during the confrontation. The confrontation which led to her attacking me first over the photographs. Uncle rewrites history and bends my reality for me in a way that makes sense, all the while I nod along.

My anger issues mixed in with her toxicity caused the whole chaotic scene. Once I realized the physical damage to her was severe, I did the better thing by covering her up so she won't bleed too much and driving her to the hospital. *Good thing I put her in the back seat and not the trunk.* Due to my messy state, I miscalculated the directions and blah blah blah… the story is bland but uncle knows how to execute it well enough to make it at least appear real, real enough for me to have a case. That's why he gets paid the big bucks.

Uncle Cliff clearly still gets paid well as his suit alone looks like it costs thousands of bucks. No wonder dad spat on my face when I told him I was studying architecture. I closed my eyes and could still remember how his spit trickled down from my left cheek and onto my new suit, tailored by my then 'lower middle class' girlfriend.

As the room filled itself with other lawyers, I followed the story I'd been told to be true, Uncle Cliff's director's cut version. I repeated everything that was expected from me and other than what was rehearsed; barely talked to anyone, like a good ole puppet. Good times.

As Uncle Cliff and his secretary convinced the authorities of how things in my life happened, I thought back to the amount of effort it took to leave dad's shadow and make a life of my own. How hard it was to actually accomplish a decent life with a career and a partner that my all-knowing father was against from the very beginning and how the inevitable, 'I told you', probably awaited me in the near future.

I opened my eyes and I'm back in the cell, then I closed them. When I opened them again I'm in front of some people, my mouth speaking in a robotic voice while my eyes bled with tears. Words it was advised to let out. I closed my eyes again when they told me to sit down. When I opened them, I'm back in the cell again, this time a different one. My life just turned into an acid trip. Not that I mind. Courtroom dramas have never really been my forte.

I'm told I'd be getting a bail. While I was there, I looked at the walls of the prison, it was as gray as cliché prison movies and I missed the pink wall I had in my bedroom. Kate's face comes to mind, not the actual face but more like the bloodied face print on the kitchen wall.

"You're lucky, you know that," Uncle Cliff lets me know. "I had just finished a lawsuit for your dad when your text arrived."

"What's he done now?" I asked as if I cared.

"Better that you don't know," Uncle Cliff said. "Better that no one knows how that man conducts his business."

We had a little small talk with some steel between us and then he left for a phone call. I looked behind me. A black man sat close by. He looked big enough to knock me out in a second. My fingers kept twitching. My eyes were wide and red. My body was alive, too awake for someone this tired. I needed to sleep and if I couldn't sleep, I'd settle for being unconscious. I don't want to be awake and aware, or even alive.

"What are you in for?" I asked. He's not in the mood for talking, which is better. He already doesn't like me. "Can I ask you for a favor?" He frowned. I gestured to him to come closer to me. It took some convincing on my part but he did. He had a rough look to him, this probably wasn't his first time here. Regardless, I did what I had to do. I spat on his face. Now I'm not racist but I did use the N-word to trigger him even more.

As expected he packed one hell of a strong punch. It helped me to focus on the pain rather than the returning memories and the rest of the chaos. It also helped me get some much needed shut eye. When I woke up the next day, I was somehow bailed out. I knew it was happening yet was still surprised at how quick it had happened. Pros of being able to get a famous lawyer, I guess. I later found out that the black dude who knocked me out also helped in more ways that I had anticipated.

Sorry man, my bad.

As I was being taken out, a nice limo arrived in front of me. *I would rather get back to the cell and wait for the hearing from there.* Since its breaking news, I wondered what my neighbors must be gossiping more about, the fact that my wife is dead or that my father turned out to be a fucking billionaire.

As the door to the limo opened, a familiar face was spotted, with a not so happy expression, which nonetheless was also a familiar expression. Déjà vu. As far back as I could remember it was always dad's favorite look. Despite the fact that it had been years since I'd seen that all wrinkled face, I still vividly remembered its ugliness. Thankfully a bunch of reporters showed up with their crew and started asking dozens of questions, so I was granted a little moment without dad in it just yet.

I didn't hear all the questions but I knew they were for me as they were followed up by a familiar name. "Did you kill your wife, Mr. Damien Jr?" "How did you find out about your wife's infidelity Mr. Damien Jr?" "Do you think this was a set up Mr. Damien Jr?" *Dave is back to being Damien Jr again.* I always hated that name, might as well call me Norman Bates, at least that one had a nice ring to it.

I got in the car with dad, who was doing his 'I'm disappointed in you' face. I looked away. Eye contact is not something my dad enjoyed anyway, especially whenever it came from me. It made him feel like I was standing above him, forgetting my place.

"I told you that bitch was trouble," I nodded, even though I couldn't care less about what the old man had to say. That bitch was my wife and one of the best things about my life until… Just because she didn't agree with everything he had to say and wasn't scared enough to voice her opinions against it, unlike me, didn't mean she was trouble. That was one of the qualities which made me love her in the first place. A bitch is annoying but a bitch that fights back with wit and truth behind her words, is hot.

"Where are we going?" I asked, fully aware that he wanted to take this sweet time to lecture me.

"Somewhere the media can't record you doing anything dumb," he retorts.

"Do me a favor and only wake me up when we're there. I'm not interested in talking at the moment, especially with you. I might as well be talking to mom's ghost," I said and lied down on the seat, awaiting the inevitable.

A sharp pain on my stomach woke me up instantly. It was a belt, my daddy's favorite disciplinary weapon, other than his boots. For half the ride, he used it to draw lines on me. I wanted to fight back and let him know I was not returning as his puppet anymore but I didn't. I let him beat the crap out of me. This time, I deserved it.

"You fucking disgrace. You have any idea how fucking embarrassing it was to hear about this mess. I told you not to marry that cunt..." he kept shouting as he knocked me to a corner. *Classic dad.* Years of history and memories were back as he treated me with his hospitality, but I just stayed there and took it. I even provoked him every now and then. It was weird how even after all this time; I could easily push his buttons. *Some things never change.*

He's older and grumpier, but also weaker so he stopped eventually. Either that or uncle decided to intervene. Whichever the case, I couldn't care less, I just wanted some silence. I could only wait for it to be over and cry myself to sleep, like when I was a child. Although I doubted I could still cry anymore.

"Get this embarrassment out of my sight," soon after, once I was able to get back on my feet, I sat and stared at him. Before he could do anything else, the car stopped. *So close.*

"We're here," uncle said, breaking the tension he clearly didn't want to be a part of, not again. We got out and I was let into an apartment that I suspected him to own. Either that or he owned the whole building.

Neither of the answers would have surprised me.

I only wonder if the poor architect went through the same shit I did. When I got my architecture degree, dad offered me my first project. I said sure. Little did I know that I would later have to change the design over and over and over. He kept demanding sillier and illogical designs. When I gently tell him that an origami bird won't work, he pretends to be dumb. More than usual. I literally went through over a hundred designs. Only for it to return to the same generic structure every building has and then never be made.

That was when I knew he did not want me to make it in the first place. I kicked myself for not getting it sooner. Before I quit his offer, I drew a new design in the shape of a dick. At the top, I dedicated it to mom. He says I was fired to this day but I made a copy of my resignation and posted it online before he had the chance. On the positive side, the other clients I had after that were a cake walk.

My room was all the way up to the 20th floor. "Take some rest and..." Uncle Cliff started to speak but I shut him off. My mind was focused on dad, or lack of him. He wasn't here with us. He was gone. I wonder whether he even took a second to think about the fact that his son just lost his wife, that despite how much he hated her, she was still his daughter in law and the better part of his son's life. The thought probably didn't even come to his mind, let alone enter his thick skull.

She may have been a cheater but at least she wasn't a beater. The unintentional rhyme made me chuckle this time, which, after the beating I just took, did not look normal. Uncle noticed that, but didn't say anything. He probably still remembers the last time he said something I didn't agree with. "You're as crazy as your old man," Uncle Cliff had said, drunk at a party almost a decade ago. "I'm not comparing you two. I'm just not good with wording my thoughts with you two," He joked, as if reading my mind and knowing my distaste for it. As a result, I punched his tooth out and made him swallow it. It was the first and last time when he compared the two of us. *Good times.* History has told him to not repeat himself ever since.

We got to my room. The guards were all ordered to stay down at the lobby and I told my uncle to keep them there as long as I stayed here. He agreed. He didn't want to talk about it or debate it, he just looked exhausted. I looked away from his tired eyes, to the apartment I was about to stay at.

It was fully designed of glass furniture, like tables, book shelves and even vases, just as modern as early 2010s magazines would tell you, only glossier and fragile. There were some paintings on the walls, a bunch of random self-help books on the shelves and a big ass flat screen on the wall.

I took a bath and wandered around this new shiny cage I inhabited for the time being. There was a new set of glasses and an iPhone on the dinner table that had a letter underneath it. I picked up the glasses and threw them right out the window. *I don't need it anymore.*

As for the letter, I ignored it, at first. Instead I searched the fridge, ate some fruits and then checked back at the table. "Call this number if you need anything," the note said. *Anything? How about a gun and some cocaine?* I called the number and it was the reception. I asked them to deliver me some big bottles of hard drinks, which to my surprise, they agreed.

One would think a father should be more controlling on drinks after the incident that just happened with his son, but then again, dad has never really cared that much ever since mom died. Come to think of it, he probably never did.

Eight

I looked around the room. It was simple yet boring, with glass all over the place, and cheap generic paintings to sell the idea of art. Even the books on the bookshelves were mostly known for just being well known. Who the fuck puts only one book from the lord of the rings trilogy but not the rest? It's for people showing off what they have but not knowing what it is.

I've been on house arrest before, but this time I *wished* for a worse outcome. I turned on the TV and as expected, the news was no longer just, 'A drunken architect murders his wife in rage'. It had turned into 'Controversial, billionaire tycoon's son arrested for manslaughter? Is he involved too in this grizzly affair?' I'd be lying if I said the newer title didn't sound better.

The drinks arrived via room service at just the right time. My neighbors were being questioned. The red head obese man from 3 floors below mine, the one with the really loud dog, was being questioned about my past behaviors while I tried to pronounce, and fail, the names of the drinks they had for me. Just like computer software, I guess alcohol gets updated every now and then too.

I imagined dad shaking his head at this news the way he did when he paid for my bail the first time. I had been in for assault. I pictured the disappointment all over his face as I started drinking. The first drink of the day, but far from being the last. *Months of rehab, all gone like a fart in the wind.*

"But why think of him?" I asked myself. "Let's do something," I looked around. "But what? What should I do? What's the plan doc?" I couldn't come up with anything. For the first time in years, my mind was blank.

I closed my eyes to see if that would help. It didn't, it just made it worse. The first face that came to me was hers, Kate's. But something's wrong. For some reason I could only picture her straight, expressionless face. I just couldn't recall her smiling or laughing, the moment I tried, my mind flashed the image of her bloodied face instead. I had a better recollection of her blood printed on the wall than of her winking at me during an inside joke.

My eyes snapped open and I looked around the room again as if I had just been teleported to some unknown place. My mind quickly redesigned the room and its furniture. I wore slippers and sat on the couch. Right in front of me was a glass table. Without thinking much I raised my leg up, froze it on air for like a few seconds and then brought it down hard on the table, shattering the glass all over the place. Some pieces of it buried themselves onto the back of my foot. It hurt but the big bottle in my hand helped. I shook most of it off like the way a dog would shake off water and picked the rest manually. My fingers painted red with blood, which I then wiped on the clean cushions of the sofa.

I wondered how much glass I could break by the time someone stopped me. I picked the pillows off the couch and stared at it. I missed the soft yellow handmade pillowcases Kate used to make. *Why did you have to do that Kate? Why? Now I can never love any other pillow ever again.* I threw the pillow across the room, like a child throwing a paper star imagining himself as a ninja. I did the same thing with the other pillow. No ninja carries just one star.

The bookshelf was next. I took out all the books and brought them to the couch as my artillery. There was not a single book I would've liked to read, that I hadn't already read. How to win friends and influence people was thrown across the room and it bounced off the TV and broke a vase before it hit the floor. *More like how to bounce off a TV and break a vase at the same time,* copyright pending.

I threw more and more books all over the place and despite not having a clear vision, was still able to hit the mark, most of the time. "I'm a fucking Natural," like when I threw the bottle at Kate's head. *Good times.*

Most of the things in the room were surprisingly delicate. It took me 3 books to break another table, 2 books to crack a window, 4 more to shatter another table and 3 more to break the aquarium that I had somehow not noticed until I made it the target. I was the *bull in a china shop.* Once the bottle in my hand was finished I used it as well and hit the chandelier on the ceiling breaking off several pieces of fake diamonds.

I thought of the man in the café, the one who had started me on this quest. He'd said, I might want to smash up my home. The thought made me laugh. He was an idiot but I guess even a broken clock is right twice a day. And if I was going to smash something, it was better if it was something that belonged to my father.

I could've lived without any of this mess but then this would've been just another one in the long list of lifeless cold rooms I had been living in for over 10 years of my early life. With clichés in the name of art and business trips in the name of traveling. Following rules to make sure I didn't make dad look bad. I've always known there are people who would kill for this, and now finally I understood them. It only took a disloyal wife and shattered dreams to get there, but hey, better late than never, I guess.

I stood on the couch, my blooded foot leaving prints all over the furry seats. I liked it. The stale clean surface finally had a unique design. But the design started to resemble Kate's face print, so I stopped looking at them. I didn't stop printing my foot all over the place however.

When I was a kid I would play with my cousin at her place. She would claim that the floor was lava and you would die if you stepped on it, classic childhood memory. I had never seen her since mom died. She was from her side and dad didn't want to be in touch with anyone who even reminded him of her.

I spent the entire morning jumping from couch to table, to chair to back to couch, making sure I didn't touch the lava floor. The hearing was in 3 days and until then, I'd be in this room, stuck, and so I figured I might as well enjoy the little things.

Given the current situation, it is hard not to think of mom. I will try my best though. But every now and then a piece of it does manage to grow and become a memory. Then that memory keeps knocking on my mind's door. Like the time mom, dad and I went to some park. But that's not important. It's just a silly sitcom that keeps recurring in my brain's television. Like usual I fight the memory off. I won.

I painted on the walls, drew a building and wrote my name under it with my own blood. I took some of the paintings off the walls. There was this one fake one with a beautiful girl dressed like an angel from some fairy tale and for a second there I felt like jerking off on it. Then I thought better of it and stopped. I just drew nipples on her and tossed the frame across the room. It landed on the kitchen table and slid all the way off it, taking down a chair with it.

I looked outside the windows and saw tiny cars and vans. They were probably full of reporters or cops. I wondered what they'd say if they could see this fancy room all broken and dismantled. I jumped towards the TV and removed it from the wall. Then I threw it as far away from one wall to the other as I could. It crashed onto the empty bookshelf and broke it into pieces. This was how I spent the day.

When room service came with the food, I ate it like an animal, outside the room, in the hallway, rather than letting any of them in. I never let them in, and judging by their expressions when they saw me walk out of my room, they probably didn't want to either. The food was great but lacked that homemade feel that I used to love about my daily breakfasts.

I should've just kept quiet about the affair.

So what if she was cheating? Maybe I drove her to it. Maybe I never deserved her in the first place. That woman didn't take shit from anyone, whereas I was dad's little puppet, back when we first met. If she was going to leave me, she would've come clean about it in the future; I know at least that much about her.

Why the fuck did I have to be a smartass and bring it up? I could have spent more time with her, the time we had left. Now I couldn't even remember how she looked when she was happy. Even my memories showed her being disappointed in me.

I picked up a new brand, this time a much smaller bottle and drank it in a single gulp. Whatever the hell it was, it was an accomplishment to finish it. My eyelids started to get heavier and I reasoned it was time for a quick break. I jumped on the bed and faced the ceiling. Within seconds I fell asleep.

Good thing I didn't need to touch the lights in order to turn them on, because when I woke up, it was evening. *How long was I asleep? Fuck it! I'm about to take one more long nap.* That was when the phone rang. *What perfect timing!* My head hurt as I looked for the phone in all the wreckage I caused earlier.

Luckily it only took under a minute to find it. It somehow ended up buried under the pile of kitchen chairs, or whatever remained of them. I was too late to pick it up so it became a missed call, but soon after, I received a text. It was Uncle Cliff, 'we have a hearing this Friday,' he reminded me. 2 days from today.

The hearing will decide my fate. I tensed up when he added, 'dad will be there'. The thousands of eyes didn't matter to me. The reporters, judge and jury were no bodies, but dad? I guess I'd have to 'behave' myself when I get there. Can't cause another scene that'll hurt my dear daddy's image in the public, a self-made billionaire for others, (who by the way was born a millionaire to begin with) a wife beater, and a cunt for people who actually knew him. Can't wait for that confrontation on Friday. *Don't worry daddy, I'll be on my best behavior for you when that day finally arrives.* Maybe I should start planning a gift too.

Uncle Cliff, along with dad, would be my ride on the given date. "Until then, don't do anything too stupid," I nodded, already going against what he just said.

"I understand. You can count on me," I replied. With the TV broken beyond repair and the furniture barely recognizable, with bloody footprints all on the floor for added measure… yeah, *I'm definitely qualified to be counted upon.*

I opened up a new bottle, again, and used the iPhone in my hand to scroll through Facebook, Instagram and literally every platform where I could find what I'd been looking for. I wanted to see pictures. Pictures and memories, of her, of my one and only, Kate.

I saw Kate every time I closed my eyes, but not as the woman I had married, but as the bloody pulp I had left behind. Now I would never get to see her the way she was. Now she was just an image on the internet. Every time I saw a smiling picture of hers, I took a sip. Soon, I was stalking my wife on social media for hours and was drunk as ever, having a Good ole time. *I am a disappointment, but I guess I just have to accept it.*

There was a picture of us she posted during our trip to France, one during her graduation where she looked the way she did the first year of our relationship, one where we were playing in the snow. I came across a picture with her parents. *Should I call them and explain to them what happened? What should I say?* Then it hit me. *Were they in court when I was arrested? Did I miss them?* The thought unsettled me, so I ignored it. Back to the pictures.

I was glad the happy faces were the only ones she posted from that winter. A miscarriage won't make for a nice post. Neither will funeral visits or arguments, or accusations and confessions.

It kind of made me wish we had also made a sex tape back in the day. We were quite horny and in love after all. To quote the great Wiz Khalifa,

Those were the days,
Hard work forever pays?
And now I see you in a better place...

Nine

One day before the hearing

I used the phone to look up one of the songs that Kate and I played during a quick dance on our Anniversary. We were in our suite, drunk as fuck. She was in her wedding dress and looked breathtaking. I was wearing boxer shorts and a tuxedo on top. *Don't ask. Just go with it.*

I held my phone on eye level with the picture of my love in her gown up high as I reminisced the times, and the moves we shared, how her hip moved, how her skin smelled and how her lips tasted. I'd taken mints to make mine taste better.

I carefully avoid the carnage on my way, nearly stepping on broken glass, again. As the song continued, I jumped over a dead goldfish and unintentionally kicked an empty bottle as I stepped on a torn piece of book cover. Harry Potter and Ron probably missed Herminie from the cover too.

However before I even got to finish the song I was interrupted by a phone call. It was from the lobby. Someone was here to meet me, the receptionist informed me. I looked at him from my iPhone's screen; he was in front of the elevator, surrounded by guards. He was bald and looked like a middle aged man; either that or the camera at the lobby was making him look like that, surely it wasn't because I was drunk. Pff.

He claimed to be one of Uncle Cliff's assistants, sent here to see me, by dad. He claimed to have all the identification and that I could call my father to check, but I didn't. I didn't want dad's new asshole puppet to tell me what to do and I certainly didn't want to ruin a nice moment I just had by calling dad. It would be like getting your dick chopped off right after an amazing blowjob.

So I granted him permission to come up, but told the guards to remain where they were. They hesitated at first but then I told them 'I knew the guy' and they backed off. He probably just needed some answers and what not, but I wasn't interested in that.

I was more interested in what he'd say once he was up here, in this mess. With the fragrance of alcohol, mixed with piss on walls and literally a piece of everything on the floor, *his reaction should be a nice fresh one.* I couldn't let any of the guards see that, they'd inform uncle right away and he'd shit upon all the fun.

It'd been a while since I met anyone, a genuine conversation with someone who wasn't a member of the staff but a puppet of dad. A former puppet and a current puppet discussing shit, sounds fun, don't it? Somehow it rarely ends up that way.

I waited for him outside the elevator as he was on his way up. By the looks of him, and considering the fact that he was sent by dad, he seemed like a well-mannered, well dressed middle aged man. The elevator doors opened, he's here.

Looking at me standing there half naked in just my wrinkled boxers and an inside out vest, his eyes were as big as an owl's. No wait, a panda's, Nah, not that either. Shit which animal was it? The one with big eyes? Ah Fuck, doesn't matter. The point is, it made me smile ear to ear like a scary clown. It was off to a good start.

"Mr. Damien Jr?" His voice was surprisingly younger than he was, or looked. I thought it was just the intercom earlier. He covered his mouth with a napkin, probably because of the smell I gave off. I hadn't changed clothes in a while, among other stuff.

"Dave," I said and offered him my hand. He was hesitant at first but he took it and as soon as he did, I yanked him towards me. He was an inch or so taller than me so it took extra strength, but I managed to force a hug, my mouth near his left ear. "Call me Dave, if you call me anything else, I'll rip your ears off with my teeth and then describe to you how they taste," a playful tease. He was taken back, afraid and unsure, but still nodded. His face screamed how he felt extremely nervous to go any further.

So far it was going great, as he followed me to my room, his mouth still covered in his handkerchief. Probably because of my body, that's what happens when you don't shower for days, yet jump around like a monkey and are covered in a mixture of sweat, piss and alcohol. *Hard work forever pays?*

"Welcome to my dungeon," I said as I introduced him to my room, or whatever was left of it. It took quite an effort for me to not crack open a smile as his eyes bounced from me to what used to be tables, chairs, sofas, TV, and everything else, including my fresh vomit on the floor which I accidentally stepped upon with my naked feet. All the while I examined him.

He was bald but not because he'd lost his hair, he had shaved. Uncle would hate that, he wished he had natural hair, which meant dad backed this guy up. Deep down I always knew dad hated Uncle's toupee but this was harsh. I looked down at his stomach. His stomach was big and ahead of his chest, it was almost like he'd been wearing something inside his shirt, a homemade WWE belt maybe. His eyes were brown and his suitcase had what seemed like a button on the side. Dad did send him; he was also probably listening and watching me from the briefcase.

"Nice gadget," I commented on the briefcase and he jumped as if I just groped him inappropriately. "Don't worry, far from being the first time dad sent someone undercover."

"Undercover?"

"Yes, I'm guessing he gave you the briefcase," he took a while to answer, and then nodded. I'm almost 1000% sure he didn't fully understand what I just said and just gave up on understanding.

"He… your father sent me to check if everything is alright. He," he licked his lips, as if he was thinking of what to say and how to say it with a straight face without looking all over the mess. "He wanted to make sure you were prepared for tomorrow."

"Well?" I raise my hands up as if to be searched. "Don't I look prepared?"

"Your father is going to kill you," he said and it sent shivers up my spine. I still managed to maintain my posture.

"Let's hope he does," I shrugged. "Pretty sure the thought has come across his mind at least once," I grabbed a half empty bottle and took a sip.

"I beg your pardon?" *Keep begging.*

"Wanna drink?"

"No thanks, I'm…" he began, but then took it off my hand anyway and gulped down a large sip. Action speaks louder than words after all. "Thanks," he gave it back.

"So what brings you here? In the land of chaos," we sat on the dinner table. Well, I did. He managed to find a chair that wasn't completely broken and sat on it. *How did I miss that one?*

"I'd like to ask you a few questions regarding what happened, with your wife," he put the briefcase on the side, the super obvious camera facing me. *Guy's an amateur.*

"Shoot," I said, my mind flashing Kate's graduation picture for some reason. She looked so confident in that photograph. I snapped back to reality as he cleared his throat, preparing his side of the words. "Wait, do I have to dress for the camera," I pointed at his case. His breathing quickened when I said it.

"Ca… Camera?" he stuttered. Jesus, he looked like he was going to need an inhaler. "No, that's just a… button, a design," he searched his pockets and to my surprise he actually did bring an inhaler. He was sucking it in.

"Relax. I'm kidding," I said and he calmed down a little. *What a clown!* "So where do we start?"

"I've been told to check your testimony and make sure it's accurate. So that we're well prepared for the hearing," that's not what he said before the inhaler, but I let it pass.

"Okay," I nod.

"I assure you that your father and uncle are working as hard as they can on your case…"

"Where do you want to start?" I interrupted him. It was getting boring. If this guy knew my father at all, he would have known the only hard work dear old dad was doing was to separate his fuck ups from mine.

"From the very beginning. Why you killed her and what you killed her with. First I need to hear your side and then compare it with what I have, to measure the accuracy," *Why don't you measure these nuts?*

"So you want the made up version, or what actually happened?" I teased getting off the table. My ass was getting too cold. He appeared to be thinking. I walked around him as I waited for his answer and then, it hit me.

"First the one that actually happened, so that we can figure out how to handle this right," *you've been caught motherfucker,* I think but don't say, even though I really wanted to. Earlier I thought he looked familiar but I dismissed it, but now, after a closer look, I recognized him.

"Don't worry; you'll get nothing but honesty from me. Every single detail you want is mandatory and I'm more than willing to provide, in like full capacity," he took a relaxed breath as I prepared my words. Before I tell him anything, I look at his face again, it looks like him but I could be mistaken. "By the way, what time is it? My iPhone's clock is retarded," he pulls out his sleeve and checks his watch, exposing his hairy forearm.

That was when I realized I'm right. He's blonde. He's not just a blonde, he's THE blonde. He was the one in the picture. Nice try Kate, but your lover, the one who you tried so hard to hide, just handed himself to me on a silver platter.

Ten

"Don't worry. This conversation is strictly off records. You can check my phone if you want to," he unlocked his phone and offered it to me. I snatched it. He's surprised, he clearly expected me to just shrug it off. The idiot was so cocky, he even unlocked it. Unknown to him I tap the alarm icon and put a timer on it that'll ring in just 20 seconds. I had my back facing him so that he would see what I just did.

"I won't worry about that if I were you," I said as I waited for my signal. "Uncle must really trust you to send you here, to me, a supposed murderer" The wait felt longer than it actually was so I moved closer to him, uncomfortable. "People in my family have trust issues so sending you here is quite a surprise," He rearranged his tie when I said it, my breath on the back of his neck. "Then again all I did was murder a filthy whore," I can sense his body tense up on the word. "A disgusting good for nothing, unfaithful lazy dirty whor…" I couldn't finish the sentence. Not because I thought she didn't deserve the compliment or because he was staring up at me with a disgusted look, but simply because I was interrupted by a loud bell noise that echoed all across the room.

He broke the eye contact once his phone started ringing. He jumped a little, as if I just stabbed him. Although the knives were pretty close by. We were at the kitchen after all, where Kate had been. I carefully picked it upside down to make sure the display remained hidden from him.

"It's Uncle Cliff," I said and pretended to pick it up. "Hey Uncle, nice assistant you sent my way," The look on his face was priceless. It went from scared when it rang, to confusion when I said it was uncle cliff, to understanding in a matter of seconds as I kept talking. "But didn't you research his background?" At that point, he was no longer hiding it. Patience was not this guy's strong suit. He knew that I knew, but I still decided to cut the foreplay for good. "Yeah, his background, he's Gerald from the same firm Kate used to work in," I said as I read the firm's official website on my iPhone and then showed him his own picture on the site, with a full set of blonde hair and a better suit. He was 9th in the top 15 lawyers of the firm according to the website. He even posed similarly to the way he did in the lipstick stained picture. "Oh and he's also the one Kate had been fucking," I stared directly into his eyes as I said it. "But we'll talk more about that when you're real," I threw his phone on the wall, missing him by a few inches, and breaking it into pieces instantly.

Now I stand in front of him, towering over him. Letting him know I had the upper hand. He stood up as well, putting us at an almost equal eye level. I wanted to stay calm, but my anger wouldn't let me. I was ready to fight, no matter what my head told me to do. This was an old fashioned standoff. For a second there I imagined us ripping each other's heads off. My fist tightened as I pictured punching him under his chin, ruining the otherwise neat jawline.

As we stared, the room fell dead quiet; the only noise was of us breathing, loud and hard. His breathing quickened but he put the inhaler on the table. *So that was an act too?* Then, with a sigh, he started to look more, relaxed, as if he was still in charge. He rested his hands on the table and looked away from me.

"I must say, for someone who drove head first onto a cop car, with a dead body still inside, you aren't as dumb as I expected," Gerald said.

"I'm not sorry to disappoint," I nod at his praise. "I wish I could say the same for you," I nodded towards his round stomach. "I saw the photos of you and my wife. I remember you being thinner. Have you been binge eating after you heard what I did to your fucktoy?" My hand shot out, grabbing his stomach. It was spongy between my fingers and I pulled it free from his waist, dangling it in front of him.

"You wore a disguise?" I asked with a chuckle. "You must be fucking mad to think I'd fall for that."

"I'll keep that in mind," Gerald nodded, admitting his mistake. *You sure will.* "So what now? You call in the cops and get me arrested for trespassing?" This guy came all the way here for a reason. Usually you won't expect your wife's lover to go through all this trouble, just to see you. *He and Kate must be closer than I thought.*

"Don't be silly; things have finally started to get interesting."

"So what do you have in mind then?" he sat back down and pulled out a cigarette. From inhaler to a cigarette? *Nice progression.*

"I'd like to know what you had in mind before you did this… act," I gestured at his stomach again. He sighed, no more beating around the bush. "I was planning on meeting you and asking you personally, about the event, about what exactly transpired that night? How things, got so fucked up?"

Is that desperation I hear in his voice?

Gerald continued. "The media either just blamed Kate and ruined her image or just talked about your father. They asked me for a quick interview but I denied them and threatened them with a lawsuit if they dared to follow me. I couldn't trust them for anything so I came to you. Knowing how fucked up your relationship with your father is, I thought it shouldn't be too hard if I played my cards right. I was right. All I had to do was mention him and you did the rest."

"Hence the disguise," He nodded.

"So you think I'm going to just spill my guts to you?" I asked.

Gerald leaned back into his chair. "I know guys like you."

"What does that mean?"

"It means you want to tell me. I can see it in your face. Why miss the opportunity to torture me with the details?"

Damn, this guy was good. "That does sound like a good idea," I said. "I'll tell you what happened. Fuck it! I'll tell you everything there is to know," he seemed pleased by the answer, at how easily I was convinced. He probably thought I was the lonely one, desperate for therapy. "But before that," I picked up his briefcase and threw it out of the window. I was not going to make it all that easy for him. "No cameras."

"There are no cameras. You just threw my lunch out," *Yeah, sure, I believe you. It's not like you were trying to trick me just a few minutes ago.* He put out his cigarette on the table and blew the last remains of the smoke at me. "Plus the whole 'recording' thing you see in the movies is wrong. It doesn't work like that. The law doesn't work the way it's shown in fiction. Even if I did decide to record this conversation, it may end up working against me for trying to manipulate the situation and forge evidence," *Now I see why Kate loved him*, they shared the passion for bragging about their law knowledge. "It won't be… authentic," *I'll keep that in mind.* Evidence has to be believable.

"Then why bother with the circus," I grabbed two bottles and brought them to the table. He took one and smelled it. "Don't worry; I'm not planning on killing you. Not yet at least," although I'd be lying if that thought didn't cross my mind. *If I kill him here and hide his body…*

"And I'm supposed to believe the man who killed his own wife," The anger in his tone was unmistakable, even if he tried to recompose himself soon after.

"I didn't plan it, it was a fucking accident," We engaged in another stare down, albeit much shorter this time. *Know your place loverboy.*

"Go on," he broke eye contact and looked around the room again. I let the silence stay for a bit longer. As expected, he doesn't like that. *How did such an impatient fool become a lawyer?* Maybe he was used to the quick back talking with other lawyers, showing off his witty side and impressing other people's wives. "I haven't been able to sleep ever since I found out."

"YOU haven't slept well? Oh poor soul," He didn't look up this time, probably realizing his mistake. He knew what he said. "Should I bring you a fucking blanket and sing you a lullaby? I might as well fart in that blanket and cuddle you to keep you warm while I'm at it," I chuckle a bit at the thought.

He stayed silent for a while. Half a minute went by before he finally spoke, "Kate deserved better," he took a sip. Maybe I really should have poisoned him.

"Sure she did. Hell, let's start knighting all the people who cheat on their partners. I'm sure Queen Elizabeth would be up for that," he looked up and stared back at me but didn't reply. He just took another sip, this time a large one. I refilled his drink like the nice host I was.

"According to your files that I've managed to read; you killed your wife, and crashed your car, with her corpse on the back seat, directly onto the cops on the side of the street. Now that's just too simple… stupid and somewhat believable in your case, but still it feels like a piece is missing. It does not feel right. That piece is not what happened on the street, neither is it what you told the cops or reporters. It's what happened, and I mean actually happened in your apartment. The confrontation, the…"

"Very well, so you want the details," I interrupted his little monologue. He didn't like it but what was he going to do about it? He just nodded again, like a puppet. "Fine," I told him everything that happened that night. I made sure to keep it as simple and quick as I can, otherwise I may have to relive it again. I got to the point where I searched her purse for her phone to call the ambulance. Then I jumped to the part where I put her in the car and drove out.

"Wait, so why didn't you call the ambulance?" *sounds like someone's been paying attention.* Before this he just kept nodding as if he was trying to convert what he had just heard into Morse code. The guy did have a thick neck.

"I did…" I looked him in the eyes as I said it. His reaction was as expected.

"Bull shit," another stare down, his desperation made me smirk. I raised my hands in a surrender move. He had caught me. So I decided to rip the Band-Aid off for him, knowing full well that his skin will follow.

"You're right. I didn't call the ambulance or the hospital, I didn't want anyone to know, or help. I broke the phone and everything else I could find in her purse, including the purse itself. I wanted her to die," It was time for the pay off.

"Why?" he was confused. I stared into his eyes as I spoke my next words. *I'm going to enjoy this.*

"When's the last time you fucked her?" he flinched at the question and broke eye contact, again. *I won this time too.* He'd been taken off guard. It took him a minute to answer but he did.

"Two weeks ago, I think. Could be more…" he looked ashamed, as one should be.

"I was going to save her but then I saw something," he was giving me his full attention and I knew immediately, I was wrong. I was not going to enjoy this. "When I was looking for her phone, I found a little item you get in department stores and pharmacies, it's called a pregnancy kit or something," his eyes grow big and for a brief moment, I imagine ripping them out of their sockets. "It showed two lines, which in case you don't know, means positive," I wondered which one of us was worse? Telling a husband that you knocked up his wife and that she was going to leave him for you was still worse than telling a father that you killed his unborn child, *wasn't it?*

"She was pregnant," the realization hit his face and then, so did my fist. The impact knocked him off his chair and onto the floor. His nose started bleeding but he barely reacted to it. How dare he turn a blind eye to his nose like that.

"We hadn't had sex in over a month. The cheating bitch had your baby in her," I wanted to fish for some knives I knew to be around as he was distracted, but then I stopped. I chuckled a little when I thought, *that's cheating.*

"You fucking monster," he lunged at me. "You killed my child," he punched me in the stomach and I stumbled, my insides on their way out. I grabbed him and with a leg behind his, pushed him down, back onto the floor again. Such a basic move yet so effective, like missionary.

I managed to get on top of him, his arms wrapped around my neck, trying to choke me. That was when I threw up. The disgusting goo fell on his face and covered his eyes. I used the opportunity to land as many fists as I could on his big ass forehead. KNOCK KNOCK, *someone there?*

Somehow I didn't see the answer coming. Surprise, surprise, the man cheated and kicked me on the groin. The irony made me groan. I rolled over the floor as he struggled to stand up. He nearly slipped on my vomit but at the last second, didn't. Instead he managed to take control of the situation. He positioned himself on top of me, sitting on my stomach and then showered me with his fists. I covered my face blocking his pathetic attempts, Laughing as I did so.

Each blow made me laugh even louder, like the way Brad Pitt did in fight club. *I am Jack's insanity,* or should I say Dave's. "None of this is going to bring her or the baby back. You lost fucker, YOU LOST," I said out loud as he slowed down. I expected him to have more stamina than that. He looked like he was going to cry and I wanted to see it. *I am Dave's lack of empathy.*

He didn't cry, but he did spit on me. It distracted me and he took the chance to land a solid punch on my nose. My nose was leaking blood as he pulled me up by my shirt. My head backwards, still laughing as he landed another one on my jaw. The blood traveled up and covered my eyes. I could barely see him anymore but I didn't care, I kept laughing. He tried to shut me up and hit me in my mouth. I pulled my arms up and covered my face again, only to start laughing again. He kept hitting me despite the block and I let him. The pain was there but so was the satisfaction, at what cost. It was a relief that I finally got to tell someone about it and what made it even better was that the special someone happened to be this asshole.

"Are you done?" I asked once he stopped pounding me, astonished that I somehow was still able to speak. *I am Dave's indestructible boner.* He was breathing heavily and I could hear him sniffle, I got my side of the answer. His side of the answer was to stomp on my knees. It hurt to stand after that. "I'll take it as a yes," I said and crawled from under him.

He was standing and could've easily stopped me, but didn't. Although he did kick the knife that was at my reach. I hadn't even noticed it there. I just dragged my body away from him and sat leaning by the nearby wall. Just like how Kate was when I destroyed her belongings. I wriggled my toes; *I can still move but should I?* I was not able to walk properly but I could still stand, which was good enough. *It's not like I was planning to run a marathon or anything.*

"I didn't kill your child," I said, working a thick tongue around my swollen mouth. "At least not intentionally. I just didn't save it either," I have no idea why I said it.

"You could've just let her go," he stood by the kitchen table and grabbed the inhaler. To my surprise he actually used it.

"Jesus, is the fucking inhaler an act or not? You smoke yet own an inhaler? Seriously," he didn't respond to my comment, it was heartbreaking.

"We could've had a life together. You could've just left her, you could've..." he made it sound like I was a bully who broke his favorite toy just because I couldn't play with it anymore.

"OR…" I screamed the word to interrupt him. I realized I too have a thick neck. "You could've just fucked someone else's wife," I paused to take a deep breath before continuing. "Hell why choose someone's wife in the first place? Couldn't you have just looked for a single one? Try online dating, there are many singles there. Or did you have a fetish for married ones?" A moment went by before he finally answered.

"I didn't know she was married back when we first met. She didn't tell me when we were going out. She confessed months into our relationship. I loved her too much to leave her by then and she assured me she'd leave you when the time was right," what he just said hurt me more than all of the fighting combined. Sticks and stones my ass, words can hurt, and they can hurt a lot.

"I loved her too you know," I said, my voice breaking a little, as I forced back my tears. I wanted to ask how long they'd been dating but I didn't dare let out the words. I was not sure if I could handle the truth.

"Well now she's dead, because of you," his accusatory tone made me want to look away but I didn't. Why shouldn't I stand my ground? He stood his ground even after her confession. He helped her cheat. I couldn't stand him after that. Maybe I should've taken the knife, and cheated too.

"She sure is. And I'm guessing your dumbass is done here," I tried to stand up, using the wall on my back for support. The scars Kate gave me had yet to be fully healed and now even her lover had piled on. They were teaming up against me ever after her death. *Perfect couple.*

"Done?" he looked at me in disbelief. "Oh, we're far from done," he got up to his feet and his next words were full of hatred and disgust. "You just confessed. I may not have anything to prove it yet but I'm not backing out until I see you behind bars forever. I'll bring the forensic reports to the hearing. Let everyone know how you let the baby die because it wasn't yours. I'll expose you for the fucking monster you are. You deserve to be in the fucking death row…" the guy had a point, I'd give him that. I just didn't care about his argument.

"Fine by me. I'll just say I wanted her to die… but once I found out that she was pregnant, I thought of helping her for the innocent baby's sake and drove her out. Maybe I'll add in court that she was probably trying to pass your kid as mine. There are plenty of whores out there who do that. There are dozens of ways I can twist this story, and become a sympathetic figure for others. All the while I ruin yours and my late wife's reputation," I snapped back, only snapped wasn't the right word. I said it rather nonchalantly. "And if you come at me, I'll expose you as the father and ruin your reputation. I'm sure your parents and your boss would be proud of your achievement and I would personally write that on your resume during the trial. I'll make you famous for it more than you'd ever be with your precious law degrees."

"YOU!!" I dodged his fist and pushed him back to the table. "I-I will…"

"You will what?" I challenged him. "Everything you do and plot, I'll find a way to counter it. Unless… unless we can make a deal," he stopped moving towards me, and didn't even try to hit me again.

"A deal? What the fuck?"

I sigh. "I'll see you at the hearing tomorrow and confess to everything in front of the judge and jury. I'll tell them exactly what I told you, but only if you do what I tell you to," I let the offer sync in. Let him be curious in regards to what I planned on doing.

"What the fuck?" he calmed down a little, he was still angry as ever but also curious, which meant he was listening and not just hearing.

"A surprise for my dad," I said as blood dripped down from my mouth. "If you agree to help, I agree to confess."

"What the fuck does he have to do with any of this? The hell has he done?"

"You have no fucking idea," I told him what I had in mind. What he had done and how I planned to expose him. I had thought of doing it alone but I could still use some company. *'A good helping hand won't hurt,'*

Kate once said, neither of us had ever dreamt of a scenario like this to use it in.

Gerald was surprised and unsure but I had a good gut feeling that I could trust him. So I did. There was nothing else to lose. "For Kate. She wasn't the only one."

Eleven

"You know, once I found out about you, I wanted to see you. I wanted to confess and apologize to you in person," Gerald said once he finished his bottle. We looked out at the clean blue sky from the couch through the broken windows. An afternoon with the man who fucked your wife… never thought it would be so… for lack of a better word, helpful.

"Apology accepted," I said but didn't mean it, and I probably never will.

"Hang on, I'm not done yet," he claimed, and then proceeded to crush the surface of his fist against my ribs. With the air knocked out of me, I fell on my knees. "Now, that's better. You'll be hearing from me soon," with that he straightened his suit, even though it was still wrinkled badly from the fight, and walked away.

"With some good news, I imagine," I joked.

"There is no good news for anyone in this scenario," *go figure Sherlock.* "I'll do what is agreed but you know you'll have to provide the evidence in a way it'll look convincing," I nodded. "Even if it doesn't work, you will still have to confess. Maybe that'll be the difference you're looking for," good idea but mine was better.

"See you around then," I remained on the floor, too exhausted to get up. I closed my eyes, thinking of what I was going to do next. I tried to take a nap but my head was too full. My mind needed to relax and my body needed to rest, so to achieve both I jerked off while still on the hard floor. The icy marble surface actually helped. This time I didn't think of Kate. I just did it.

The next morning, I called in room service to clean up all the mess. To make it look exactly how dad would want it. My back was killing me as I got dressed. *Sleeping on the floor was a bad idea.* Let's not focus on that though. Let's pull all the attention back to the plan. Let this be a show people will never forget about the great business tycoon Mr. Damien.

I begin the day by not getting drunk, shocker I know. I brushed my teeth and even used mouth wash, thankful to my past self that he didn't include all the bathroom stuff during his throwaway rampage. Once I got fresh, I started cleaning. The room was a huge mess, so I couldn't do it alone.

Room service came and cleaned up the place while awkwardly sneaking glances at me as if I was a fucking psychopath, especially the ladies who cleaned my vomit, piss and the rest. *Can't blame them.* Even as I was helping them, I was constantly thinking how dumb I had been.

I got dressed in a black suit with a white shirt. I looked like John Wick, except with less hair. Either that or I looked like an extra waiting to get killed in a john wick movie. Regardless, I did a little stretching, only to regret it right away. It was hard to walk straight but I managed to avoid looking like a hunchback.

Next step was to wear some perfume. After the nice hour long bath, I felt fresh and tidy, *kinda forgot how it felt to be clean for a change.* With all done and me looking like how a normal human being should look, I took another deep breath and looked out the window. The press outside was waiting for dad's inevitable arrival and so was I.

"Speak of the devil," dad's car arrived and I got a text immediately after.

"Get your ass down here, now," the text said and I replied soon after.

"As you command, Sir," I waited for the elevator to get me all the way down, while in my mind I rehearsed my future actions. Surely I could do this. Even after all these years, dad was dad. Highly emotional and simply predictable.

As expected the hallway was packed with reporters and guards. To think only 5% of this was available to me on other days, just because dad wasn't around, it was… logical, I guess.

"Mr. Damien Jr today is your hearing, how are you feeling?" a reporter asked me in a hurried tone. *She's freakishly tall.*

Uncle Cliff was there trying to answer some of their questions by not directly answering any. I slipped from under some of the giraffes, also known as bodyguards, and stood in front of her. Seeing how I wanted to talk, they surrounded me, I'm like a magnet. The first time I'd managed to get more attention than dad, but then again, that was mostly because he was still inside his car. *Wuss.*

"Call me Dave," I paused before adding, "I feel ashamed for my father, whose self-made reputation is no longer as respected because of me. I feel embarrassed that he has to go through such a shameful event because of me," I spoke my rehearsed lines, that sounded generic at best and remained as such as the conversation went.

"What happened to your face?" a man yelled his question from all the way back. I'm surprised that wasn't the first question I got asked, I even had a line prepared for that.

"The first rule of fight club is, you do not talk about fight club. Next question," I shout back. *I am Dave's cockiness.*

"Do you regret what happened to your wife?" another one asked and I wanted to slap his Sherlock cap off but instead I just stared blankly at him. I closed my eyes for a sec before replying.

"Of course I do. She was the love of my life and I wanted nothing more than to be with her, but sadly, history tends to repeat itself."

"What does that mean?" I found an opening and made a run for it.

"Uncle Cliff will answer your other questions," I pulled him by his fancy brown tie and made him stand closer to me and the press. "I'm going with dad, alone," I whispered in his ear. He shook his head in disagreement. I pulled him back towards me. "If you come anywhere near the fucking car, I'll rip that toupee off," I said it in a matter of fact way, the way he'd known to be true. "This is between me and him," I brush by him and get into the back of the limo, with dad. *Time for our long awaited reunion.*

"What the fuck happened to you?" His face was blank. His tone was one of irritation. Was it too much to ask for a little sympathy? Then again if he'd shown a normal human emotion, I wouldn't trust it anyway.

"Had a fight with Irony," I said. His mood always turned when given vague answers, especially me. *The spark.* I passed by him, to the driver of the car.

"What's that supposed to mean?" I ignored his question as I knocked on the small window between us and the driver. The driver was old and alone.

"Does the phone in the back work?" I asked. The driver frowned at that. It was a stupid question after all, but still one I needed to ask.

"It works if you know how to use it, if that's what you're asking?" I closed the small window between us and went back to my seat.

"Who're you calling?" dad asked. He's annoyed already, good. This may be easier than expected.

"No one," I called my apartment. The red record button looked unused. Time to take its virginity today. It never hurts to have a backup. All it took was a single ring and he picked up.

"Yeah, I'm here. We're prepared. We've managed to get you over ten minutes," Gerald told me. Ten minutes? It was more than enough. I wondered how he pulled that off, no wonder Kate loved him.

I cut the call short and then dialed the same number again. And this time I pressed the record button on my side too. The answering machine was not a bad purchase after all. *You've reached Kate and Dave, we may be busy at the moment, so please feel free to leave a message right after the beep, thank you for calling,'* her voice. My heart skipped a beat when I heard that soft charming voice of hers.

I wanted to cut the recording and call back again, just to hear it all over, but that would've made him suspicious. It took all my strength not to break down. I remembered all the failed attempts she made before this. I hoped the machine kept all those too but at this point it was just wishful thinking.

"You know I don't like you talking like that," Dad's anger was apparent in his voice, and it helped me shift my attention to him instead.

"I just wanted to hear her voice one last time, through voicemails," my tone sounded more desperate than I wanted it to. I had planned something else to say, but her voice changed it. *Time to improvise,* like I used to do back then. *Good times.*

"You are pathetic," I put the phone on the side, away from his sight but close enough for him to be listened to, and recorded. *Here goes nothing, or was it everything?*

"I know," I sigh. "I guess, I missed her more than I thought. She deserved better."

"You really think that?" He asked, daring me to actually admit it.

"I do."

"Then you're a fool. People like them deserve to be punished. They deserved what they got," I guess it's time I mention mom.

Twelve

"She got what she deserved. That's what happens to whores like her," I keep my hands near the receiver and block the phone with my body. This way if he tries to reach for it for some reason, assuming he can even see it, I'll be there to stop him. *He can be really unpredictable sometimes.*

"You would know about that, won't you? After what happened with mom…"

"Don't mention her," he hisses. "She's a forgotten part of our lives and deservingly so."

"You know, I try. I try to forget her but this one memory just keeps hanging around my mind. Of a picnic."

"I don't want to hear it," he says but his voice is softer, more emotional. It was time for exploitation. For the entire hard exterior he makes it up to be, his softer side also existed at one point, and mentioning mom always worked. I felt grubby for bringing mom into this. She didn't deserve to be mixed up in my scheme, but I didn't have a choice.

"It won't take long," he doesn't object, even though he pretends to be annoyed. Like me, he wants to hear it but pretends otherwise. "In this memory of mine, mom, me and you, we're like, walking on a picnic spot. We're lost, on a hill."

"Yeah, I know that one. Your dumb mother spent the whole day forcing us to walk around like idiots," I let out a chuckle. He does remember. Maybe my incident forced him to recall his. *Even better.*

"I remember you complaining. Not as often as you would after the… incident, but still. She kept reassuring us that she knew the way. She was determined to prove to us that she knew what she was talking about. Kinda makes sense why you married her," his face twitches at that. "All day following her on foot. She kept saying she knows the place, to trust her, to be patient. That we were behaving like whiny little children. At the end after 3 hours of non-stop walking, she finally gave up. She did not know the place."

"She didn't do shit like that," Dad adds.

"Excuse me?" This wasn't part of the plan.

My father stared out of the window, his shoulders falling, a faraway look in his eyes. It was the first time I'd seen him anything other than angry.

"Is there something you're not telling me?" I asked.

Dad sighed. "Your mother, she didn't give up. She found a place we already circled back to, for the 3rd time and told us this was the place," He gestured through his hands. "She wouldn't accept the fact that she was wrong. That she didn't know better. Fuck, she couldn't even pronounce the name, yet claimed it to be where we were supposed to be the whole time."

"So," I sigh, this time for real. "So you're telling me, that the one memory I constantly recalled of my mother all these years, isn't even accurate?" my voice breaks a little. *I really liked that memory.* I can't lose focus. This story can still be used to get to the point.

"No one told you to think about her in the first place," *change of plans.*

"Fuck you!" Time to cut to the chase. Enough foreplay.

"Excuse me?" he's pissed.

"Fuck you, you don't tell me what and who I want to think of. She was my mother."

"Her greatest achievement, No doubt," he snapped back.

"She was the best part about my childhood. A childhood full of an alcoholic father and…"

"Mind your language."

"She didn't deserve you in the first place. You never loved her. You only married her to fuck her and hated her for not being just another sex toy."

"Shut up!" The lies mixed with hard truths make up for one of the deadliest cocktails.

"You only ever wanted her to be under your control," he's breathing heavily. "No wonder she wanted to leave you for someone better."

"She wanted to leave me because she was a cunt. I gave her everything. That woman couldn't do anything. A toddler had more talent than her. That woman couldn't make you a cake even if her life depended on it. She wasn't skilled at anything…"

"Maybe you should've married a cook then."

"Believe me, the picnic was just the start of the problems I had with that woman. I bought her everything she ever wanted," He ignored me and kept talking. "I canceled millions worth of meetings when she went to labor. I spent hours of sleepless nights at the hospital when you were born. To make sure I was there to provide her with everything I could. Both of you almost died in the hospital. And what did I get?" his voice gets louder as he speaks of the things I never knew he did. I'm not sure if I believe him. He can be a pretty convincing liar sometimes, but I'm not sure if this is one of those times.

"You got what you deserved. Just because you were there for her then, doesn't give you the right to treat her like trash and beat her, let alone kill her," I'm surprised he hasn't lunged at me yet. Maybe because he knows without uncle around, I may not hold back this time. I probably won't.

"You don't know a damn thing," my father shouted.

I felt the temperature drop in the car, but I wasn't ready to back down yet.

"Tell me, then," I shouted back. "Tell me why you did it."

My father slammed his fist into the car window so hard I was surprised it didn't smash. "I killed her because she was a whore. I caught her fucking the gardener, on my… on our bed. I trusted her. You have no fucking idea how much I loved her. She didn't love me. Hell she didn't even love you."

"Take that back," I said. That went too far.

"You have any idea how often I would come home from work to find you outside in the pool, or in the rain, on the mud, nearly getting pneumonia twice. Once I came home and found you crawling next to the fireplace. You had burns on your forearm," I don't remember any of it. *Pros of being a toddler.* "You were lucky the maid found you, otherwise those marks will still be on you. Does that sound like a good childhood?"

"Still better than getting whipped with a belt for hours over bunking a day in school," he ignores me. I don't blame him. It was a weak comeback.

"The day I caught her, you were 8, playing with a kitchen knife, A KITCHEN KNIFE. You won't remember," *the worst memory I have.*

"I remember what you used that knife for, once you took it from me," I paused before adding. "Do you?"

"She got what she deserved. That's what happens when you don't care about the people who love you," His voice broke.

"You get stabbed and buried in the backyard, right under the doghouse. Right?" I looked down, unable to meet his gaze anymore.

"She had her chance to run," he said rather defensively and recomposed himself. "Instead she helped the asshole escape. She was begging me to kill her at that point. The asshole didn't even come back to save her. It broke my heart to do it but she deserved it."

"I don't believe you. I don't believe you have a heart."

"I used to. Until that gold digger decided to crush it under her feet."

"And you decided to bury her alive for that," my face red with anger. Not because I had to relive the worst memory of my helpless young life but the fact that destiny decided to repeat itself on me. I keep asking myself, *am I going to end up as bitter as him too?* If so, it's good that I don't have a child.

"At least I didn't get caught with her corpse," he remarks, I nod. *Your greatest achievement.*

"No, no you didn't. It's been like 20 years since then? Sometimes I wonder if there's a statute of limitations on murder," I said. I should have asked Uncle Cliff about it when I had the chance.

"Who cares?"

"I do. I didn't want what happened to you to happen to me."

"Well it did, didn't it? Maybe we're not that different after all," I don't want to believe that. That's the last thing I ever wanted.

"We are," he lets out a chuckle at that.

"How?"

"I'm willing to accept what I've done. I'm not a coward like you."

"You're stupid then," his confidence was speaking for him.

"We'll see about that," I stop the recording and wait for the text. 'We got him' Gerald lets me know.

After a few minutes I get another text from him, letting me know he's on his way with the police.

The recording is convenient but can also pass as a genuine accident, and what's better, it's related to an actual crime scene. *This can still count as evidence.* And to my luck, a few days later, it did.

"Mr. Damien, I'm afraid you're under arrest," *That escalated quickly.* I've been dying to hear those sweet words.

Thirteen

I did it. I confessed and not just for me. I confessed for mom's sake, for being useless then. It felt great to be able to let all of it out for everyone to hear. The media gasped when I mentioned mom getting buried alive. Someone in the audience even said, 'Poor woman'.

The only sad thing was that Kate's parents were also there, in the courtroom. I couldn't even look them in the eye after what I'd done. When I saw them, I remembered my wedding vows and how they had turned out. I also learned that a homicide is not an answer to infidelity, a lesson that screams *better late than never*. I hope dad learned it too but I doubt he will.

Once mom's body was found, or what remained of it, dad's image took a nosedive down. Out of nowhere his secretaries, house maids came up, exposing his real personality to the media. Some even accused him of harassing them sexually. The biggest surprise to me was that the whole recording, while taken into consideration, was still not that discussed. Turns out my confession did most of the work. Having said that, the recording did end up helping the world see where I got my violent tendencies from.

Regardless, I've done my part. He's going through his set of court proceedings and all his lawsuits made sure he drowned in media coverage. Mission accomplished, but then again, at what cost?

Right now, I'm in a cell, serving my sentence. Every now and then,

Uncle Cliff comes to visit me. I asked him for a small favor, to bring me a family album from my place. It took him a while but he did. Better late than never.

I flip through the album and notice that I've put Kate and mom's pictures together in one of the pages. I stare at the image as I rub my chest with the heel of my palm.

I wonder if they got to meet each other in the afterlife and if so, how it must've gone. 'Oh hey, your son killed me for the same reason his father killed you,' mom will be like 'Oh fuck! I guess it's a family tradition now,' it sounded too animated and silly but I can't help it. I no longer remember how they actually sound. Yet just the thought of them together discussing the irony, brings tears down my cheeks and I burst out laughing.

Author's Note

I hope you enjoyed it, reader. I had this story in my mind for a while. I originally wrote this as a short film for my older cousin. He directed it, as another cousin and I acted. We sucked at acting and he was even worse at directing, and so the idea was scrapped entirely. Back then it was just the scene with Gerald and Dave, with a completely different outcome.

During the lockdown however, I had some time off work and since I was tested positive with the virus, I was quarantined in my room the whole time. *Yay me?* That was when I decided *I want to write*. I didn't know what I was going to write, only that I wanted to write.

So after some thought, I decided to revive this old idea and added new things to make it more coherent. As I wrote, the story grew and the character motivations and interactions changed. It took me about a week to finish this book's first draft, but I didn't publish it for months, thinking this wasn't good enough to be published, to be seen by anyone. I hope I was wrong.

Please let me know of your thoughts and opinions through your reviews and ratings, and please feel free to be honest. I'm still very new at this and want to improve my writing skills more.

Thank you for taking some time to read my work and I hope I was able to make it worth it. If you'd like to know about my future projects, or if you want to read a free short story, scan the QR code below.

New Address

Adam has been struggling to make ends meet and cope with the trauma of his past. Living with his father, mother, and sister in a lower-middle class neighborhood, Adam's hatred for his cousin and uncle, the ones who have caused him so much pain, intensifies when they decide to move away. But when a new tenant, Howard, moves in, Adam is met with a conflict he never expected. As Howard interacts with Adam's sister, Kathy, and her mother, Helen, he finds himself becoming more and more attached to them. Little do they know of the feelings Howard is concealing and the danger it will bring to the family.

In "New Address," readers are taken on a thrilling journey as they explore the dark depths of family trauma and secrets. If you enjoyed the heart-pounding suspense of "Gone Girl" or the exploration of family dynamics in "Where the Crawdads Sing," you'll love this gripping novel.

What follows are the opening chapters from my Debut Novel, "New Address"
I hope you like it.

PROLOGUE

Blood poured out of his busted lips and his bruised chin. From there, it traveled down to his chest, as young Adam tried to move his mouth away from under his cousin's knee. He was a fat man, four inches or so shorter than Adam, but unlike him, much bigger, and for now, stronger.

He had used his strength and size against Adam many times before. The fat ass didn't used to be this violent. That was because Adam was too naïve then to realize the difference between pranks and abuse.

Once Adam learned the difference, he started to fight back. His cousin took his retaliation as an excuse to cause harm. Fight fire with fire, fight slaps with punches and kicks. He used his weight as a weapon and sat on Adam or walked over him any chance he got. Sometimes, he jumped on him when he was distracted. As if barging in his room wasn't uncomfortable enough.

Back then, Adam was skinny as a beanpole and not very strong, but he was fast. So, he used that to his advantage. Fat people were slow and took their time doing things—such as getting up off the ground. One of his knees was on Adam's face, the other was on the floor balancing the rest of his body.

Adam had been on the living room couch when his cousin decided to jump on him and bury his knee in Adam's face. He didn't want to be in this apartment, but Dad was determined Adam was going to do things his way—whether he wanted to or not. Dad wanted his son to be a man and not a pussy that ran from a fight.

Adam kicked the one standing knee and as expected, his chubby cousin collapsed onto the floor. Adam took the opportunity to spit in his eyes and kick him in his face. Humpty Dumpty fell on his back. Before he could get up, Adam ran across the hallway to his apartment. Dad was across the living room playing cards with Uncle when the fat bastard had attacked Adam.

Adam didn't ask Dad for help. He knew he wasn't going to get any. Especially with Uncle sitting right next to him. Both playing the same old card game, with Uncle even wearing the same old green leather jacket. Dad would swallow a stranger's semen before he swallowed his pride. Adam caught his father's gaze, and the man looked away as if disgusted by his own son. Mom was at the doctor's with Kathy who had caught a persistent cold. Not that her being here would have improved matters by much.

Mom knew exactly what went on in their house but was powerless to stop it. All she could do was treat the wounds. She only helped him get through it, not stand against it. Adam wasn't surprised. People like Mom—spineless—couldn't stand for herself, let alone tell others to do so.

Mom only ever suggested to him to avoid things. He promised himself he would avoid it when he could but if something came to him, he would also fight it. If Dad was going to use "boys will be boys" or "be a man" as an excuse to let his son get beaten, Adam was going to turn it around and feed all of them those very words over and over.

The fat ass was on his feet. Adam sprinted across the hallway to his apartment. The worst part about his cousin, other than his abusive nature, was that he lived right next door. Adam reached his apartment and looked back.

His cousin stood next to the door, his arm leaning on it, his stomach rising up and down as he smiled. He didn't walk, he limped. Adam slowed down once he reached behind the door and stood there. For a second, he thought he may take on the fat fuck, but the moment didn't last long.

His cousin wiped the blood and saliva off his eyes and licked it off his fingers as Adam watched. Adam slammed the door, so he wouldn't have to look at that face. The slam woke Damian up and he came to Adam's aid. Adam picked the bulldog up and took him to his room. The only company he wanted by his side.

Dad stayed with his uncle and cousin for as long as they let him, which meant hours. So, Adam finally had some time to kill. If only he could actually kill. If he could get away with murder and had a good enough excuse, he knew who his targets would be. But he also knew the gift of strength was not on his side—yet.

He wouldn't be this weak for long however, Adam knew that much. Once he hit puberty, he would grow taller, even if a little more. He would be stronger too, and then he would make them all miserable. He wouldn't break that promise. He washed the blood off his face and thought of the steps he needed to take. Get a job. Get athletic, become not only a man but the man of the house. He would make Dad the pussy. Then he'd strike his uncle and cousin. He'd make each one of them pay no matter how long it took.

Years later, Adam was at work when his uncle and cousin moved out. By the time Adam got back home, the apartment next door was empty. A sight that would have pleased him years ago, now disappointed him. Adam needed someone to fight, to argue, to insult. Who would take the brunt of that frustration? His father.

Howard

It was time to move on. It was time to move in general. Howard and Sarah had just moved to this new apartment, temporarily. His house was about to be painted. He couldn't stand the color—the colors Cate's mother chose for the house before her death.

The same colors he and Cate painted together all over the house, only for his 9-year-old to leave him too. What good is a million-dollar house if everyone dies in it before making enough memories?

Sarah suggested selling the place. She took the thought back when he didn't answer. On one hand, it has the loss of two people Howard loved most in his life. On the other hand, it also contained some of the best memories he ever had. Cate's mother, Jane, died giving birth to an angel. Then that angel died of cancer before she even got to live a full decade.

Feels like just yesterday Sarah and Cate were getting to know each other. They had met for the first time during Cate's fourth birthday. Sarah and Cate liked each other from the start, and it was enough. *Things are about to get good,* he had thought when he saw them smile and play together. Everything would be fine. He was wrong.

Sarah was trying to be as helpful as she could while stuck in the tiny apartment. She was in the hospital consoling Cate in her last hours. It must've hit her just as hard, yet here she was, trying to smile as much as she could to make him feel better.

Howard nodded along with his wife's happier disguise, faking it together, as if his daughter had died years ago and not months. As if her memories didn't haunt him every single day.

An older man walked out of his apartment across from the one Howard was about to rent and glanced in his direction. Their eyes met. He smiled awkwardly; Howard returned the gesture. Before either of them could let a word out, the man walked away. Only he did not walk—he sprinted.

Howard shrugged it off. He had other things on his mind, like the door for example. It was the same size as the door to Cate's room. He shook his head; he knew he was overthinking again, it was just a door after all. They were all the same size. Even the one he lived at before he sold his business was the same size. The only difference is the lock. The old one had a weaker lock, one that could be opened by a credit card. Otherwise, they all mostly consisted of the same things—wood, hinges, nails, and a small gap underneath—only in here, they had a somewhat larger gap.

The gap between the door and the floor in his house was small enough to slide things through. He used to slide in all sorts of things. Like movie tickets, a slice of cheese on paper, stickers, and birthday cards etc. Here, he could slide in two check books stacked on top of each other at once. He used to slide things from under Cate's door. She used to do the same for his door. It was their thing. A thing neither of them could remember how it started, a thing he was going to miss. One of many things that won't happen anymore the way it used to.

One of the worst things about loss is that whenever you think things are getting better, an old relic of a memory comes in to disturb the peace and remind you of what you lost. Howard especially hated how suddenly, yet consistently, these memories were intruding. They had been invading his mind for months, to the point he struggled to both stay still, and move around. A change needed to be made. Luck already made its move, now it was Howard's turn. So, he moved.

"Rent is due at the end of the month," the property owner, Miss Griffin said. They shook hands as the movers moved in boxes and the rest of the furniture. Howard inhaled harder and for longer when he saw Cate's laptop table. It had a sticker of the *Powerpuff Girls* on it. He looked away.

Sarah noticed and pulled him closer. Howard tried to act calm and kissed her forehead before looking around the apartment again. He remembered the last time he had been in an apartment like this. He was alone, playing video games on his computer, games he made. Back when he lived in a place like this and met Jane for the first time. It felt like a century ago. Maybe living with Sarah will be similar, but hopefully with a different outcome.

He looked back at the boxes and noticed Cate's shoes. The moving company probably mistook it for one of Sarah's shoes and brought it here. Howard had purposely bought bigger shoes just so he could keep the receipt and give it to Cate when she grew taller. It was supposed to be a silly surprise from her silly dad. She never got to wear them. Now it's a shoe too small for Sarah, and the storeroom was where it was going to stay. He did not have the heart to throw it out.

"Is it okay if we go out for dinner tonight?" Howard said, not wanting to stay among all the things. Too many memories flooded him. Sarah agreed and they went out half an hour later. As they prepared to leave, Howard strolled around the rooms some more. They were going to live here for a few weeks, maybe even months if he needed to.

He had chosen the apartment online, in hopes to have some of his younger, stronger, and more determined days back, however long it may take. Whether or not he would get his old model optimism back was yet to be seen.

Scan this QR code to get to the rest of the Novel